Two Tailed Trouble – A Norwegian Forest Cat Café Cozy Mystery – Book 4

by

Jinty James

Two Tailed Trouble – A Norwegian
Forest Cat Café Cozy Mystery – Book 4

By

Jinty James

ISBN: 9781696495257

DEDICATION

For Annie and AJ

CHAPTER 1

"No more murders, whoo-hoo!" Lauren Crenshaw held up her hand to high-five her cousin.

"No more murders, boo-hoo," Zoe returned glumly.

"Brrt?" Annie, Lauren's Norwegian Forest Cat, trotted up to them.

"I thought we could celebrate the fact there haven't been any murders for a while, Annie," Lauren told the silver-gray tabby. She looked quizzically at her cousin.

"I know murder is wrong – and horrible." Zoe shivered. "But it was fun sleuthing around with you and trying to discover who the guilty party was."

"I understand," Lauren replied. And she did. So far, in the small town of Gold Leaf Valley, there had been three murders that she and Zoe had helped solve. But it had also been nice not to worry about suspects, or wonder if every customer who came into the coffee shop was a killer.

Lauren and Annie ran the Norwegian Forest Cat Café in the northern Californian town. Lauren had inherited it from her grandmother, as a regular cafe. When Zoe had visited, she, too, fell in love with the place, and had eagerly accepted Lauren's job offer.

Annie led the customers to the table she chose for them, Lauren baked the cupcakes, and Zoe acted as her right hand. A couple of months ago they'd recently attended an advanced latte art class, and now decorated their customers' lattes and mochas with swans and peacocks, as well as the usual hearts, rosettas, and tulips.

The interior walls were pale yellow, and the furniture consisted of pine tables and chairs – today, the chairs stacked on the tables. A string-art picture of a cupcake with lots of pink frosting decorated one of the walls – evidence of Zoe's latest hobby.

"Right now, we're involved in catering for the twentieth anniversary of the local senior center," Lauren reminded her cousin.

"Are all the cupcakes frosted?" Zoe's expression brightened. "I could do some."

"I only have a couple more," Lauren replied quickly.

Zoe was a whiz as a waitress and made a pretty good latte, as well as having a zest for life that sometimes Lauren envied. But frosting a cupcake generously but neatly, without getting into a sticky mess, was not one of her skills. Sometimes Lauren had a difficult time avoiding splodges of frosting on her apron when she iced them, and Lauren was the resident cupcakc baker.

"Okay." Zoe nodded. "You are going to put some aside for us, aren't you? I'm loving your new recipe – white chocolate cherry – mmm."

"Thanks. One each for us, and one for Ed when he comes in tomorrow," Lauren replied.

Ed was their baker – his pastry was featherlight and legendary in the small town. But he stayed in the kitchen where he didn't have to interact with customers.

"Oh, good." Zoe grinned.

"Brrt?" Annie asked, looking up at them. Her green eyes looked impossibly cute and imploring.

"I don't think cupcakes are good for cats," Lauren said gently. "What about an extra helping of chicken in gravy for dinner tonight instead?"

"Brrp," Annie grumbled, then sighed. Although the café was closed on Mondays, she'd decided to accompany them while Lauren made the cupcakes, and Zoe made herself a latte.

"What time should we head over to the senior center?" Zoe asked. "I can't believe this is our first catering job, can you?"

"So far everything's gone well," Lauren said, not wanting to jinx anything. Making two hundred cupcakes hadn't been as time consuming as she'd thought. And it had been fun coming up with a new recipe – she'd wanted to create something to celebrate the fact that the local senior center had been operating in the town for the last two decades. A white chocolate cupcake with white chocolate frosting and a maraschino cherry on top seemed fitting.

"Maybe we should have a mocha," Zoe suggested a minute later. She drummed her fingers on the counter. "So we get an extra caffeine fix before tonight."

"I'm okay. But you have one."

Zoe hopped off the wooden stool and started grinding the beans. The aroma of chocolate and heady spice tantalized.

Lauren almost regretted her reply, but reminded herself she'd already had two lattes that morning. She did not need another one. She just hoped tonight would go smoothly.

Maybe frosting the last couple of cupcakes would help calm her.

"I'll be in the kitchen for a few minutes," she told Zoe over the hiss of the milk wand.

"No worries." Zoe focused on creating as much micro foam as possible and barely looked up.

Lauren walked into the clean kitchen.

On the large bench were two hundred cupcakes – only two remained to be iced.

Lauren grabbed the bowl of frosting from the large refrigerator and set to work, careful not to leave a sticky mess on her apron.

"There," she murmured, surveying the result with pride. The sweet treats looked delicious. She hoped she'd made enough – although they'd been informed there would be around fifty guests tonight.

Taking off her apron, she washed the frosting bowl – not that there was much left in it. Now all they had to do was pack up the cakes and load them into the car.

"Have you finished?" Zoe poked her head through the swinging kitchen door, her brunette pixie bangs springing upward. "I'm caffeinated and ready!"

"Yes." Lauren joined her cousin in the main area of the café.

"Brrt?" Annie stood up in her cat bed and stretched, her spine arching.

"We're going home now," Lauren told the feline.

"Brrt!" Annie hopped out of her bed and trotted to the door that guarded the private hallway. The passageway led to the attached cottage, which Lauren had also inherited from Gramms. Not only was Zoe her colleague, she was also her roommate.

Lauren unlocked the door, watching Annie scamper down the short hallway. She shimmied through the cat flap and disappeared into the cottage.

If Lauren was right, Annie would be sitting next to her food bowl.

"I'm coming," she said, unlocking the door and walking into the kitchen. "Chicken in gravy?" Lauren asked, opening the refrigerator.

"Brrt!" Annie weaved back and forth next to her new lilac food bowl, her long plumy tail waving.

"I did promise an extra helping." Lauren smiled as she spooned out the food. "I'm sorry you can't come with us tonight, but I think there'll be too many people there. They'll all want to pet you and talk to you, and it will be very overwhelming for you."

"Brrp," Annie replied in a muffled voice as she concentrated on eating her dinner.

Maybe that was why the cat had been a little grumpy that day – she was upset at missing out on the party tonight.

Although Annie seemed to love her role at the café, interacting with the customers and leading them to their tables, Lauren was careful that she didn't get overtired. And tonight, with a lot of seniors vying for Annie's attention … Lauren shook her head. No. She had to do what was best for Annie.

"Now all we have to do is have an early dinner and head over to the center," Zoe said.

"What are we going to eat?" Lauren stared at her. "I haven't organized anything for our dinner. I've been so busy thinking about cup—"

"I hear you." Zoe nodded. "Which is why I made us sandwiches. And we've got our white chocolate cherries for dessert."

"Good thinking," Lauren said gratefully. She'd also been daydreaming about her boyfriend, Mitch. They'd been dating for a couple of months now, and everything had been going well.

"So when do you think Mitch can set me up on another blind date?" Zoe asked as she slapped turkey and cranberry sandwiches onto white plates.

"Brrt?" Annie asked, having finished her meal.

"Zoe wants to go out on a date," Lauren informed the cat.

"Ooh, maybe we can double!" Zoe's brown eyes sparkled.

"Do you think that's a good idea?" Lauren asked doubtfully.

"Yes! Because if the guy turns out to be a dud, then I've still got you to talk to."

Zoe's foray into internet dating several months ago had not gone well. Until recently, she'd channeled her energies into exploring new hobbies, such as knitting, crochet, and string-art. Mitch had introduced her to a couplc of his friends on the police force, but Zoe hadn't seemed to click with them.

"The two guys you met weren't duds." Lauren frowned. She'd appreciated Mitch trying to help.

"No," Zoe admitted. "But I didn't have anything in common with them. And they were so serious!"

"Serious can be good."

"Yes, but not all the time," Zoe replied. "I don't think either of them knew how to smile!"

Lauren tried to hide her own smile. Zoe had a point. When Lauren had met them, she'd wondered if either of them were a good match for Zoe. Her cousin had declared both dates a total fail.

"I'll ask Mitch," Lauren said.

"It's okay, I'll ask him."

"All right." Lauren stacked the plates in the sink and checked her practical white plastic watch. "We'd better eat our dessert and get going so we've got enough time to set up."

"We should have loads of time," Zoe declared. "I bet some of the seniors will want to help us, anyway, so they can sneak a peek at the cupcakes."

"You could be right." Lauren bit into her dessert, the white chocolate in the frosting and crumb tantalizing her tastebuds with its sweet creaminess.

"Brrt?" Annie jumped on the kitchen chair next to her and placed a paw on Lauren's plate. *Can I have some?*

"No." Lauren shook her head. "We've already talked about this."

"Didn't you get an extra helping of chicken?" Zoe chimed in. She took a huge bite of her cupcake.

"Brrt," Annie replied in a downcast manner. It sounded as if she'd rather have a cupcake for her dinner than chicken in gravy.

"I'm sorry." Lauren gently stroked the silver-gray tabby. "We shouldn't be home too late tonight. I'll tell Mrs. Finch and Hans you said hello."

"Brrt!" Annie sounded a little cheerier. The two seniors were among her favorite customers.

Lauren and Zoe quickly did the dishes, then locked up.

"We won't be long," Lauren told the feline.

"You could play with your toy hedgehog," Zoe suggested.

Annie's ears pricked up and she trotted toward the living room.

They walked to Lauren's white compact car parked outside. Although October, the day had been warm. The evening sun made her glad she'd decided to wear her usual work outfit of pale blue capris and an apricot t-shirt.

After a short drive they arrived at the senior center, a one-story tan brick building with an attached carport and smooth green lawn, set on a large block of land. It wasn't as busy here as the main street, where their cat café was.

"Only two cars were parked in the lot – a gray sedan and a dusty blue compact. The carport sheltered a pewter-colored minivan.

"Where is everyone?" Zoe asked. "The party's tonight, right?"

"I'm sure of it. I double-checked the date." Lauren turned off the ignition. "Let's start unloading the cupcakes."

"Okay." Zoe hopped out of the car and opened the trunk.

They took a box each and walked over to the entrance, an open stained-glass door featuring orange and gold autumn leaves.

"Hi, Lauren, and Zoe." A short man wearing a blue and white polka dot bow tie smiled at them. He appeared to be in his sixties, and wore a navy suit and white shirt to go along with the neckwear. The jacket almost hid his slight paunch. "Come in, come in."

"Thanks," Lauren replied.

"I'll show you where to set up." He led the way down a brightly lit hallway to a large room decorated in ruby with cream accents.

"You can put the cupcakes over there." He gestured toward a large wooden table covered with a cream tablecloth standing at one end of the room. Paper plates were stacked on top.

"What kind did you bring?" he asked, his blue eyes twinkling with curiosity.

"White chocolate cherry," Zoe announced. "Wait until you taste them!"

"They sound wonderful."

Lauren opened one of the boxes.

"They look wonderful too." He beamed. "Thank you, girls. I'm sure our members will enjoy eating them."

"What about the coffee?" Lauren asked.

"Oh yes, I'll bring the urn out in a minute, as well as cream and sugar. If you two can serve the cupcakes and the beverages, that will be a big help. There are always last-minute things I need to do at functions like this."

"Happy Anniversary." Lauren smiled.

"It's great that the center has been running for twenty years," Zoe remarked.

"Thanks. Tonight we're having a special guest – the new owner of the property. I'm hoping he's going to give us another generous lease – Mr. Lapton, the previous owner, was very good to us."

"What did he do?" Zoe asked curiously.

"He rented it to us for a low monthly fee, and didn't mind what improvements we made to the building. When we first started the center, this building needed a lot of work – that's why the rent was so low. But with our members all pulling together and volunteering, as well as their know how, we slowly improved the building. Now the landlord could rent it for many times more than we pay each month."

"You've been here from the beginning?" Lauren asked.

"Yes, as well as a few others. I'll let you in on a secret - I'm going to retire in a few months and will hire my replacement. I'll still be a fixture here – but as one of the members instead of the director!" Barry chuckled.

Lauren and Zoe finished setting out the cupcakes.

"We've got more in the car," Lauren told him.

"I'll set up the beverage station for you." He rubbed his hands together and walked out of the room.

"I didn't know about the special guest, did you?" Zoe asked in a low tone as they headed toward the car.

"No. Which makes me extra glad I came up with a new cupcake flavor for tonight."

"He's sure to like it – they all will," Zoe reassured her.

They made quick work of bringing in the rest of the cupcakes and arranging them on large silver platters.

"They look amazing," Zoe declared when they were finished. The maraschino cherry on top of each cake glistened in the overhead lighting.

"They do," Lauren admitted. She could be very critical of her own baking efforts, but Zoe was right.

A large stainless-steel coffee urn now sat at one end of the table, along with paper cups and stainless-steel teaspoons.

"I feel guilty about all this paper waste." Barry bustled into the room. "But it's just not practical using real cups for tonight. If someone gets a little wobbly and drops their cup, it means extra cleaning up as well as making sure nobody cuts themselves on one of the shards."

"You're right." Lauren nodded.

"But we always use real crockery at our senior meals," the director continued. "Did you know about our lunch special? It's on every day for people over sixty."

"No, I hadn't heard about that," Lauren replied.

"That's because we're not sixty yet." Zoe nudged her. "We're not even half that age."

"Of course, of course." Barry nodded. "But perhaps you know someone who does qualify? It's a fun way for the seniors in our community to make new friends and enjoy a quality meal. It only costs three-dollars-and-fifty cents for two courses."

"Goodness," Lauren murmured. There was no way she could compete with those prices.

"I hope you won't put us out of business," Zoe joked.

"People love your cupcakes," Barry told them earnestly. "Our members are always talking about your coffee, Ed's pastries, and of course, Annie." He peered around the room as if expecting to see the Norwegian Forest Cat. "You didn't bring her with you?"

"She wanted to come," Lauren told him, "But I thought it would be too much for her with so many people here."

"I completely understand." He looked at his silver watch. "Our members should be arriving soon."

Lauren and Zoe turned on the urn and Barry departed, saying he wanted to be ready to greet the first guests.

"Hello." A woman in her fifties poked her head around the door. "How's everything going?"

"Fine," Zoe said cheerfully.

"That's good to hear." The woman entered the room. She wore a tailored sleeveless white top and smart fawn slacks. "I'm Denise, Barry's assistant."

"Oh, I didn't realize." Lauren exchanged a glance with Zoe. Barry hadn't mentioned an assistant.

"I'm only part-time." Denise laughed. "Barry likes to think he can run this place himself, and for the most part he can. But sometimes I think he forgets that I exist." She shook her head. "That's men for you."

"Oh, yeah," Zoe replied. "They can be really weird, can't they?"

"Definitely." Denise nodded. She scanned the room. "It looks like you've got everything under control. Did Barry tell you about our special guest?"

"Yes," Lauren replied. "He's the new landlord, isn't he?"

"That's right. And we're all hoping that everything goes smoothly tonight, so we can impress him. If he's in a good mood, it might influence him to write a new lease with the same favorable terms."

After a couple more minutes of chit-chat, Denise left to pick up some of the members in the minivan.

"Not much pressure then," Zoe joked.

"I wonder why they didn't tell us about their VIP guest," Lauren mused.

"Thank goodness we – you – outdid yourself with the cupcakes," Zoe said. "Not that you wouldn't, anyway."

"Thanks." Lauren smiled at her cousin. Zoe was her biggest cheerleader. She just hoped she was Zoe's.

"I don't know what else we can do until the guests arrive." Zoe looked around the room. "There are plenty of chairs over there so people can sit down."

"And a trash can at the end of this table."

"So there shouldn't be any waste for us to dispose of later," Zoe said. "Hopefully."

"There you are, dears." An elderly lady with a walking stick tapped her way into the room. Two spots of orange rouge decorated her cheeks and her dusty pink lipstick matched her cardigan, which was teamed with a beige skirt. She peered at them through her wire-rimmed spectacles. "Where's Annie?"

"Hi, Mrs. Finch," Zoe greeted her cheerily.

"Annie's staying home tonight," Lauren said apologetically. She knew how much Mrs. Finch doted on the cat. The senior was one of their favorite customers, and she was one of the four members of Zoe's knitting/crochet/string-art club. The others were Lauren, Zoe, and Annie.

"We thought tonight might be too much for her," Zoe added.

"I understand." Mrs. Finch nodded. "Please tell her I'll be at the café tomorrow."

"I know she'll be pleased to see you." Lauren smiled.

"Would you like a cup of coffee?" Zoe asked.

"There's also soda." Lauren gestured to a couple of brightly colored bottles. "Or water."

"Coffee would be lovely, dears," Mrs. Finch said. She looked at the cupcakes. "Is that a new variety, Lauren?"

"Yes. Would you like one?"

"It's white chocolate cherry," Zoe chimed in.

"One would be perfect," Mrs. Finch replied. "But I think I need to sit down."

"Of course." Lauren hovered by her side as the elderly lady sat on a nearby chair.

"Where's everyone else?" Zoe asked as she presented Mrs. Finch with a cup of coffee. "I put some cream in it for you."

"Thank you, dear." Mrs. Finch's hand wobbled as she took the cardboard cup. After taking a sip, she said, "I must be early."

"How did you get here?" Lauren asked curiously. Mrs. Finch usually walked to the café, but she only lived one block away. The senior center was farther than that.

"I took a taxi," Mrs. Finch admitted.

"We can give you a ride home," Lauren said.

"We have to clean up afterwards, though." Zoe wrinkled her nose. "That's the part of catering I don't like. It will be fun to drive you home though, as long as you don't mind waiting for us to finish up here."

"That's very kind of you." Mrs. Finch beamed. "But I don't want to put you to any trouble. Barry said he could drive some of the guests home in the minivan, so I might take him up on his offer."

"That's nice of Barry," Lauren commented.

"He's so helpful." Mrs. Finch took a sip of coffee. "And the lunches here at the center are very tasty." She looked distressed as she realized what she'd said. "Not that I don't enjoy your cupcakes and pastries, Lauren."

"It's okay," Zoe said cheerfully. "We can't compete with a three-fifty lunch."

"The center gets funding," Mrs. Finch told them. "That's why the price is so low."

Lauren presented the elderly lady with a cupcake.

"Thank you, dear."

"Hello, Lauren, and Zoe." A dapper German man in his sixties entered the room.

"Hi, Hans." Lauren smiled at him.

"I see I am not the first." He greeted Mrs. Finch with old-fashioned good manners.

Zoe and Lauren gave Hans a cup of coffee and a cupcake as well.

"Everyone should be coming in now," Hans informed them. He looked around the room. "No Annie? *Ja*, it would be too much for her, I think."

"Yes," Lauren replied, glad that he understood.

Suddenly their group of four became eight, then ten, then fifteen. The members of the senior center continued to stream in until Lauren was sure there were fifty guests, just as Barry had promised them.

"I hope we've got enough cupcakes," Zoe whispered to her.

"There should be at least three each," Lauren replied, "even if more guests arrive."

"Phew." Zoe scrutinized the gray-haired guests. "Do you think they could all eat so many?"

"I think we're going to find out." Lauren watched as an elderly man with a pot belly snatched up his second cake.

The buzz of conversation grew louder as a few more seniors arrived. Lauren and Zoe manned the refreshment table, doling out the coffee and sweet treats.

"Coming through. Watch out!" A lady with curly gray hair pushing a rolling walker approached the table at a fast clip.

Zoe stepped in front of the table to greet her. "What can we get – ow!" She hopped on one leg and rubbed her shin, glaring at the senior. "You got me!"

"Sorry." The older woman didn't look very apologetic. "I told you to watch out. Once I get going with this bad gal—" she patted the black metallic frame "—I have problems stopping in time. Maybe she needs better brakes."

"What would you like?" Lauren asked. She glanced at Zoe. "Do you want to sit down for a bit? I can handle things."

"Yeah." Zoe limped to a spare chair nearby.

"I'll have one of those cupcakes," the speed demon said. "And a coffee. With a lot of cream. And two sugars. I like it sweet." She winked at Lauren.

"I'm Lauren. Zoe and I run the Norwegian Forest—"

"—Cat Café. Yeah, I know. Everyone talks about your cat," the senior said. "Pretty good idea, doing the catering for us, and drumming up business for your coffee shop." She narrowed her eyes. "Where is this cat that everyone talks about?"

Lauren explained again why Annie had been left at home. She was also glad she'd decided not to bring the feline. Right now, the hum of conversation was a lot louder than at the café. The seniors were laughing and talking with each other, some sitting down, and others standing in little groups.

"I'm Martha," the curly-haired woman said as Lauren handed her the coffee. "I come here nearly every day."

"That's nice," Lauren said, not sure what else to say. In her peripheral vision, she saw Zoe still rubbing her leg and glaring at Martha.

"You bet it is." Martha grinned. "I get a good hot meal for cheap, and there's lots of things to do. Bridge, gin rummy, poker, movie afternoons, dancing. We even tried line-dancing last week. And there's plenty of gossip to catch up on as well."

"Really?" Lauren asked.

"Uh-huh." Martha gulped her coffee. "We even talk about you younger folk.

Everyone knows you're dating Officer Hottie."

"Don't you mean Detective Hottie?" Zoe interrupted, coming up to stand next to her.

"Ha." Martha looked at Zoe, as if taking her measure. "I stand corrected." She rummaged in the basket of her walker. "Let me write that down." Martha pulled out a small notebook and pen.

Lauren blushed as Martha scribbled in the book.

"What about you?" Martha demanded of Zoe, putting the notebook back in the basket. "Where's your hottie, a zippy gal like you?"

"Nonexistent." Zoe suddenly looked glum.

"It'll happen, hon." Martha patted Zoe's shoulder. "Don't you worry. Just give me the word and I'm sure us old people can rustle up a nephew or a grandson for you – one that will definitely give Detective Hottie a run for his money."

"Thanks." Zoe brightened a tad.

Martha munched on her cupcake, then spotted someone she apparently knew. She waved to another gray-haired senior and spun the walker around.

"Gotta go, girls. There's gossip to be had over there!" She sped off in the direction of the other woman.

"I wonder what Mitch would think about her." Zoe gestured to Martha, now halfway across the room. "Would he like being known as Detective Hottie?" She grinned.

"Don't go there." Lauren shook her head. Knowing people were talking about her love life wasn't that amusing.

"They can talk about your boyfriend all they like, as long as they're not feeling sorry for me and my dateless existence."

"Martha's right," Lauren told her. "I'm sure it will happen for you."

"Let's hope so. Or else I might take up Martha on her offer!"

A couple of minutes later, Barry clapped his hands, asking for quiet.

"Welcome, everyone. I've just had a text from our special guest, and he'll be arriving in a couple of minutes. I'm sure you're all thrilled as I am to welcome him to our center."

A grumble of murmurs greeted his announcement.

"Some of them don't look too happy," Zoe whispered to Lauren.

Denise, Barry's assistant, joined him in the center of the room.

"Barry's right," she told the crowd. "We must make a good impression on Mr. Ralph Lapton, so he'll write us a new lease with the same favorable terms."

"How are you two doing?" Father Mike, the priest of the local Episcopal church, approached Lauren and Zoe.

"Good." Zoe grinned at him.

"Would you like a cupcake?" Lauren gestured to the remaining cakes. "There are some left."

"I'd love one." Father Mike smiled. "Thank you."

"Have you just gotten here?" Zoe asked. "We haven't seen you until now."

"That's right." The priest took a small bite of cake. "I gave Ms. Tobin a ride."

"She's here?" Lauren exchanged glances with Zoe. Until a few months ago, Ms. Tobin had been their prickliest customer. That had changed recently, when Lauren and Zoe had warned her that she was being scammed online. The older woman's personality had softened, and now they were no longer on their guard when Ms. Tobin entered the café. But at times, her prickliness could still surface briefly.

"She's over there." Father Mike motioned to the other side of the room. Since Barry's announcement, the seniors had resumed their conversation with each other, but now Lauren could pick out words such as "lease" and "new landlord".

Ms. Tobin stood with another woman, who looked a little older. Ms. Tobin was tall and slim in an amber skirt and short sleeved cream blouse. Her friend had graying blonde hair cut in a soft bob and wore a white and cornflower blue striped dress.

Lauren waved, and Ms. Tobin smiled and waved back.

"I didn't think Ms. Tobin was old enough to be a senior," Zoe said. "She's not sixty yet, is she?"

29

"I don't think so," Father Mike replied. "But I do know her friend is a little older than her and attends the activities here."

A commotion at the door drew Lauren's attention. A man and woman entered the room.

He seemed to be in his late forties, with the hint of a belly straining his expensive looking indigo shirt. His thinning dark hair was plastered back from his forehead and his chin looked a little jowly.

His companion appeared to be in her early thirties. Her strawberry-blonde hair was styled in a flattering layer cut that framed her heart-shaped face, while her shapely figure was sheathed in a figure-hugging emerald gown.

"Welcome, welcome!" Barry rushed to greet the couple. After a few seconds of conversation with them, he turned to address the crowd.

"Everyone, this is Mr. Ralph Lapton, and his wife Crystal - our special guests!" Barry looked expectantly at the seniors, as if waiting for them to applaud.

Denise started clapping. Most of the others joined in.

"Would you like to say a few words?" Barry asked Mr. Lapton.

"Thanks for inviting us." Ralph Lapton's voice was hearty. He glanccd at the refreshment table, his gaze zeroing in on the cupcakes. "Save some for me, hon."

Crystal nodded and walked over to the table, reaching for a paper plate.

"I can get them for you," Lauren murmured.

"Thanks." Crystal smiled briefly.

Lauren picked up the tongs and selected four cupcakes – two each for Crystal and her husband. She offered the glamorous woman the plate.

"Is that enough?"

Crystal glanced at her husband and then back to the plate. "He's supposed to watch his cholesterol, so yeah, that should do it."

"Would you like some coffee?" Zoe stage-whispered.

"No. But some water would be good."

"No problem." Zoe poured two cups of water.

"I have a big announcement to make." Crystal's husband's voice boomed out.

"I've got plans for this place. My grandfather was an idiot, leasing this land to you for peanuts. Next month, when the old lease expires, I won't be renewing it. Instead, I'm going to knock down this place and build a resort!"

Cries of "No!" and "How dare you!" echoed through the room.

"What?" Barry paled as he stared at Ralph. "You can't do that."

"Yes, I can." Ralph grinned, clearly pleased with himself. "There's nowhere decent to stay in this town. I'm going to change that."

"There's the motel," someone called out. "It's been here for years."

Ralph snorted. "That dump? You couldn't pay me to stay there."

"There's been talk for years about a large motel being built on the outskirts of town," a woman spoke. "This town isn't big enough for one new motel – let alone two!"

"You must be speaking about me." Ralph chuckled. "I've decided to forget about that plan and focus on developing this site. You're right, this town isn't big enough to sustain two of my developments. One will suit me just fine."

Lauren glanced at Crystal. The other woman looked embarrassed as she nibbled on a cupcake.

"You can't take our center away from us," Denise told him, a militant glint in her eye.

"That's right." Barry glared at him. "We've built this place practically from scratch. Our members have pitched in over the years, donating their own time, labor, and know how. This was a ramshackle building when your grandfather leased the land to us, which is why the rent was so low. We've been here twenty years!"

"You tell him!" a couple of people called out.

Angry murmurs filled the room.

"The town is going to benefit from this," Ralph told them. "All the store owners will increase their customer base. You might get more visitors to your senior center from the people vacationing at my resort."

"But we won't have a senior center," Denise fumed. "You're taking it away from us!"

"You can find another building," Ralph said dismissively.

"Or," Zoe spoke up, "you guys could crowdfund and buy this place from him!"

"Yeah, we could do that!"

"What's crowdfunding?" a frail looking lady asked.

"That's certainly an idea." Barry looked gratefully at Zoe. He turned to Ralph. "As director of this center, I'm formally asking you to give us some time to raise the funds to buy this property from you."

Ralph shook his head. "Sorry." He didn't sound sorry. "It's a done deal. I've already got business partners lined up to make this happen. As soon as the lease expires, we'll be breaking ground."

"Don't you need permission from the planning commission?" Denise asked.

"Yeah, that's right," a stout man called out. "You can't just do whatever you want these days."

"I've been told that won't be a problem," Ralph replied smoothly.

"He probably bribed them," Lauren heard someone mutter.

"We're going to object!" Denise called out.

"Yeah!" a few elderly men shouted.

"It won't do you any good." Ralph shrugged. "I still won't be renewing your lease."

"Let's try and turn this into a constructive discussion, everyone." Father Mike strode up to Barry and Ralph. "Gold Leaf Valley is a small town. Do you really think people will visit your resort?" His voice was earnest.

"Hell, yeah." Ralph grinned. "I've got friends in the tourist industry and some of them run bus tours for old folks—" he looked at the crowd, "—just like you. My resort is going to pack them in every day of the week!"

The seniors drew in an audible deep breath, as if they were one.

"This happened to the town where my friend lives." Martha smacked the handle of her walker. "The town was never the same. Too many tourists made some of the locals pack up and move elsewhere."

"Save Gold Leaf Valley!" someone cried out.

A lot of the seniors took up the chant.

"Save Gold Leaf Valley! Save our senior center!"

"I told him not to do this." Crystal still stood near Lauren and Zoe. She looked at her plate, seemingly surprised that she'd eaten two of the cupcakes. "He thinks he can do whatever he wants."

"I hope things don't turn ugly," Lauren murmured to Zoe.

"Maybe we should pack up the remaining cupcakes before a food fight starts." Zoe replied.

"Good idea."

"Everyone!" Barry clapped his hands for silence, but the chanting was too loud for him to be heard. He grabbed a chair and stood on it. "Everyone!"

The seniors gradually quietened when they noticed their director's antics.

Barry drew in a deep breath.

"I don't think arguing with Mr. Lapton is going to achieve anything tonight. Why don't we all go home and see if we can come up with some solutions?"

Father Mike made his way to the middle of the room.

"Barry's right. Why don't we pray for a solution tonight, and tomorrow we can have a meeting about this in the church hall?"

"Good idea," Denise, Barry's assistant, called out.

"What about six p.m. tomorrow?" Father Mike suggested.

"Sounds good to me." Barry nodded. "Before you leave tonight, please write your name down if you'd like a ride to the meeting tomorrow. The more members who attend, the better."

"It won't do you any good." Ralph snorted. "It's my land. I can do whatever I want with it."

"We'll see about that!" Martha waved a fist in the air.

"Yeah!" A lot of the seniors cheered.

"You're going to be sorry, young man!" a frail woman with sparse platinum gray hair warbled. She grabbed her companion's arm, as if calling out had been a big effort.

"Maybe we should leave." Crystal walked over to her husband. "You can eat these in the car." She shoved the plate of cupcakes toward his stomach.

"These folks might have more to say to me." Ralph grinned, seeming to relish the distress he'd caused.

"I think your wife is right," Barry informed him. "I don't believe anything can be achieved tonight."

"You're welcome at our meeting at the church hall tomorrow," Father Mike said. "Perhaps we can all come up with a compromise."

"Nice try, Father," Ralph scoffed. "But I don't believe in compromise. I already told you people – it's a done deal."

"I'm going." Crystal gave her husband a sideways glance. "Are you coming or not?"

"Not yet." He looked at his watch, which had an unusual purple glass face that complemented the yellow gold casing.

Crystal tightened her lips, then stalked out of the room.

"What do I have to do to get a cup of coffee around here?" Ralph demanded.

"The refreshment table is over there." Father Mike gestured toward Lauren and Zoe.

Ralph headed over to the table.

"What have you girls got for me?" He eyed Lauren and Zoe speculatively.

Lauren bit back the impulse to be rude to him. Zoe wasn't so restrained.

"I don't think you'd like what we've got," she told him. "It's percolator coffee. And all the cream's gone." She made a show of lifting the lid on a white china bowl and peeking inside. "All the sugar's gone, too. You'd have to have it black."

"Hit me." He grinned, as if relishing the little power play.

"Okay." Zoe shrugged and poured him a cup of black coffee. "Here you go." She placed the cardboard cup on the table.

He eyed the last few cupcakes while snatching up the cup. "How about some more of those?"

"Sorry," Lauren replied. "There's a two-person maximum. And you're already holding yours." She couldn't believe she'd just said that.

"Yeah," Zoe added. "Only two per person." Her tone made it sound like a tragedy.

"What happens to the left overs?" Ralph asked as he bit into his cupcake. "I bet you two take them home and eat them." He grinned, white chocolate frosting staining his lips and teeth.

"If you must know," Zoe said loftily, "we give them to the church, to help feed the poor people in the area."

Lauren looked at her cousin in admiration. Why couldn't she fib like that? They usually didn't have many left overs, as she and Ed baked fresh cupcakes and pastries daily.

But Zoe's lie was actually a good idea. She'd discuss it with her after tonight.

The developer garbled something as he sank his teeth into the half-eaten cake.

"Lauren, Zoe, we're going to call it a night." Barry approached them. He ignored Ralph. "If you two could pack up, I'll start giving my members a ride home. Denise will be here if you need any help. Oh, and feel free to keep any cupcakes that are left over."

"No worries," Zoe said cheerfully.

Relief rolled through Lauren. After what had happened tonight, she couldn't wait to get home.

"Come on." Zoe nudged Lauren. "Help me with the urn." The two of them carried the coffee maker to the kitchen. Judging by its light weight, the developer must have drunk the last cup of coffee.

"I hope the new landlord's gone when we go back into the party room." Zoe shuddered. "I don't like him."

"That was a clever excuse for not giving him any more cupcakes," Lauren told her. "And we should think about doing that – offering Father Mike any leftovers for people in need."

"That man doesn't deserve to taste your cupcakes," Zoe said fiercely. "I can't believe he wants to kick out the seniors and build a monstrosity."

"I know." Lauren nodded. She'd never expected tonight's events to turn out like they had.

"We'll have to help them find a new home," Zoe continued.

"Perhaps Father Mike can come up with a solution," Lauren suggested. "Like using the church hall."

"That might be the perfect solution," Zoe enthused. "Except when there's another event on – doesn't a needlepoint group meet there every week?" She shuddered. Zoe was not known for her sewing skills.

"Perhaps the seniors could join in." Lauren hid a smile at Zoe's reaction. Her cousin enjoyed trying out new crafts – apart from anything that involved sewing.

"We'd better go and pack up the rest of the stuff." Zoe patted the urn. "Now we've taken care of this thing."

When they entered the room, Lauren felt the energy had changed. Now there was a small, subdued crowd, talking in murmurs.

Lauren scanned the room.

"I can't see Ralph," she whispered to Zoe.

"Good!"

They stacked the remaining unused paper plates.

"He's gone, girls." Father Mike came up to them. "I don't think he was prepared for so many members to argue with him, persuading him to change his mind."

"Coward." Zoe snorted.

Lauren exchanged a glance with her cousin, who nodded. "Would you like to take home the left-over cupcakes, Father? Maybe you know someone who could use them."

"That's very kind of you." The priest smiled. "Thank you. I'm calling on a couple of elderly people tomorrow – I'm sure they'd enjoy them."

"We'll pack them up for you." Lauren grabbed a cupcake box and placed the six remaining cupcakes inside, before handing it to him.

"Are you two coming to the meeting tomorrow?" he asked.

"Wouldn't miss it," Zoe told him cheerily. "We'll be finished at the café by then."

"I just hope we can come up with an acceptable solution – for everyone," Father Mike said. He thanked them again for the cakes, then left with a couple of seniors.

Lauren and Zoe continued to pack up.

"Just about finished, girls?" Denise came over to them.

"That's right," Lauren replied with a smile.

"Barry asked me to give you a check for tonight." She handed Lauren a little white envelope.

"Thanks. I hope you were happy with everything."

"Are you kidding? Your cupcakes were divine, and having you two serve the guests meant Barry and I could circulate and chat to everyone, as well as attending to last minute things. It was worth the money."

"We're happy to handle another event for you," Zoe spoke up. "Just let us know."

"We definitely will. But I'm not sure if there will be another one, if Ralph Lapton gets his way. Where will the seniors go if we lose this place?"

"The church hall?" Zoe suggested.

"That's definitely an option," Denise replied, "but we wouldn't have all day and evening access to it, the way we do with this building. And I don't know how we'd manage the catering for our senior lunch special. We have that every day of the week."

"Isn't there a small kitchen in the church hall?" Lauren asked.

"Yes, but I don't know if it will be big enough for our needs," Denise told her. "One of our members used to be a chef and advised us on what we would need in order to cook for a large number of people."

"That's impressive," Zoe murmured.

"Our members come from all walks of life," Denise replied. "We have hundreds of years of experience among our members. And it's certainly come in handy more than once."

"Like electricians, and doctors, and—"

"Lawyers!" Zoe snapped her fingers, interrupting Lauren. "Do you have any lawyers? They could advise you on what to do about—"

"Sadly, no." Denise shook her head. "Archie used to be an attorney, but he passed away last year. I don't think any of our other members have worked in the legal profession, which is a bit of a disappointment right now. We could certainly use their expertise."

"What a shame," Lauren sympathized.

"Perhaps Father Mike will come up with a solution at the meeting tomorrow," Zoe said.

"I certainly hope someone does," Denise replied. "I don't know what our members will do if we're kicked out of here."

Lauren and Zoe finished up. They waved goodbye to Denise, who was speaking to Martha and a few other seniors.

"Phew!" Zoe blew out a breath as they walked to their car. A few overhead lights shone on the small parking lot. The blackness of night surrounded them. "I can't believe that all happened!"

"I know," Lauren replied with feeling.

"Maybe we can come up with some ideas before tomorrow night."

"I hope so." Lauren unlocked her car.

"Hey! We could have special senior rates, like half price specials when it's our slow part of the day," Zoe enthused. "Especially on Tuesdays."

"That's an idea," Lauren replied. "But shouldn't we have the same special for everyone, no matter how old they are?"

"Good thinking." Zoe nodded. "Let's do it next week! I'll make a poster and put it in the window."

"You're on." Lauren smiled at her cousin.

They got in the car and Lauren started the engine.

"I think I'll just go straight to bed when we get home."

"Me too," Lauren replied. All she wanted to do was curl up with Annie and tell her about tonight, glossing over the unpleasant bits.

Lauren drove out of the gates and down the road. Even with her headlights on, the darkness forced her to drive slowly. Only an occasional streetlight lit the way. She didn't want to hit a rabbit or other wildlife darting across the road.

Zoe chatted about the next knitting/crochet/string-art club meeting, to be held at Mrs. Finch's house on Friday evening. She'd been very enthusiastic about string-art for the last two months, while Lauren had struggled to finish her knitted scarf. Zoe had already tried knitting and crochet, and had grown bored with both crafts after a short while. Lauren wondered if her cousin would stick with string-art, or would try something else soon.

"What's that?" Zoe pointed at a large, dark object looming in front of them, at the start of a deserted side road.

"Is it a car?" Lauren slowed down even more. Had someone broken down?

There weren't any houses nearby, just grass and bushy trees.

She turned into the side road and pulled up alongside the object.

"It is a car. A fancy sedan," Zoe said. "Look, the driver's door is open!"

Lauren braked. The other car's headlights glowed in the darkness.

"We should check it out." Zoe unbuckled her seatbelt.

Lauren reached into her purse for her phone and turned it on, just in case they were the ones who would need help.

"Maybe we should think things through first," Lauren told her cousin. "There's no one around. What if it's some kind of trick?"

Zoe paused. "You're right. But what if someone's hurt and their phone isn't working, or they don't have one with them?"

"We should call the police." Lauren held out her phone.

"Is this an excuse just to hear Mitch's voice?" Zoe teased, then sobered. "You're right. Call 911 and then we can investigate."

Lauren raised an eyebrow at the order, but pressed the buttons on her phone. She didn't think Mitch had any plans for the night, but she decided to call the local police station, instead of her boyfriend.

The officer who answered said they would send someone out right away, and to stay on the line. Lauren relayed the message to Zoe.

"Cool. We can check it out for them and we'll be safe because we've got law enforcement on the other end of the phone."

"Okay." Lauren took a deep breath and got out of the car the same time as Zoe, her hand glued to the phone. Sometimes she thought she was overly cautious, but at other times, like right now, she thought she was just the right amount of wary.

But Zoe was correct – what if someone was injured?

"Hello?" Zoe called out as she shut the car door. "Is anyone there?"

"Ma'am, what are you doing?" the officer on the phone asked. "I'm advising you to wait in your car until the police arrive."

"I understand, but what if—"

"Lauren!" Zoe's voice sounded panicky. "I think he's dead!"

CHAPTER 2

Lauren rushed to her cousin's side. Zoe's finger pointed to a long lump in the middle of the road. The abandoned car's headlights shone weakly on the form, making it hard to see if it was a man or a woman.

Zoe fumbled for her phone and pressed the flashlight app. A white beam of light highlighted the body of a man.

Not just any man – it was Ralph Lapton! His blazer and slacks were rumpled and his expensive looking watch was smashed, a purple glass fragment lying on his belly. The time on the watch read 9.35.

Lauren's words tumbled over themselves as she told the officer on the phone what they had discovered.

"We have to wait in my car," she told Zoe.

Zoe nodded, shaking.

Lauren towed Zoe back to the car and bundled her into the passenger seat.

"Here." Once Lauren was inside the vehicle, she rummaged in her purse and gave Zoe a mini chocolate bar. She grabbed one for herself and popped it into her mouth.

"Thanks," Zoe mumbled around the dark chocolate, seeming to come back to her normal self. "I need this."

"We're okay," Lauren spoke to the officer on the phone. "I've locked our car doors."

"Good," the reply came. "Help will be there in a few minutes."

"Thank goodness we're not in the middle of nowhere," Zoe said thickly, as she swallowed the rich cocoa treat, "but it sure seems like it."

"Yes." Lauren closed her eyes as she savored the last of her chocolate. Why did the dark of the night make things seem more sinister? She glanced at her watch – 10.20. She wouldn't have hesitated stopping to check out the broken-down car in the middle of the day – would she?

"What was he doing here?" Zoe asked. "And where's Crystal?"

"She left before him, remember?" Lauren said. "Maybe he had a flat tire, got out to have a look, and—"

"BAM! He got run over."

"Yes."

They fell silent for a few moments.

"Maybe now the seniors won't have to worry about losing their center," Zoe mused.

"Do you think Crystal won't go ahead with the plans to build a resort?"

"If she inherits, maybe the seniors could appeal to her," Zoe replied. "She seemed nicer than her husband."

"She did," Lauren said thoughtfully.

"I guess we won't know until the reading of the will. I wonder when that will be?"

"It's none of our business," Lauren told her.

"*He* made it our business." Zoe pointed through the windscreen at the figure lying on the road.

Just then, car lights flashed and a police vehicle pulled up behind them.

"I wonder if Mitch came out," Zoe said.

"He's off-duty," Lauren said. In the rear view mirror she could see another car approach. It looked like Mitch's.

A lean and muscular man in his early thirties approached her window. She rolled it down, awareness fluttering through her at his dark brown eyes and short dark hair.

"Are you okay?" he asked gruffly.

"I'm fine. So is Zoe."

"Chocolate helped." Zoe nodded.

A slight smile crossed his lips.

"What are you doing here?" Lauren wrinkled her brow. "I thought you were off-duty."

"I am. But the station called me and said my girlfriend had reported a body."

Her face warmed.

"You two are so cute." Zoe grinned.

"Do you know who it is?" Mitch asked, ignoring her cousin.

"It's Ralph Lapton. He was at a party at the senior center tonight."

"Where you were catering." Mitch frowned.

"Yes. He's the new landlord."

Lauren saw the uniformed officer approach the body on the road and check for vitals. He shook his head at Mitch.

"Did anything unusual happen at the party?" Mitch asked.

"Oh, yeah," Zoe replied. "That man wanted to tear down the senior center."

***

Mitch drove Lauren and Zoe home, explaining that Lauren's car would have to be checked out. "So we can rule out you and Zoe right away," he explained, looking a little embarrassed.

"You don't seriously think we ran him over, do you?" Zoe demanded. "Maybe someone did, but it wasn't us."

"I don't think that," Mitch replied, "but everything has to be done correctly."

"I understand," Lauren told him. Right now, she was too tired to feel miffed about it, although she understood Mitch was just doing his job – even when off-duty. Still, it had been good of him to come out to the scene and check that she and Zoe were okay.

Once he pulled up outside her cottage, Zoe hopped out of the backseat. "I'll give you kids some time alone." She grinned.

Lauren watched her cousin saunter up to the front door of the Victorian cottage, Mitch's headlights illuminating her path.

"Are you okay?" Mitch asked.

"I'm fine." She turned and smiled at him, his light citrus scent teasing her. "Thank you for checking on us tonight."

"Anytime. You know I don't want anything to happen to you."

"I don't want anything to happen to you, either."

"I'm a trained police officer – and a detective."

"And I make cupcakes and coffee." She sounded rueful.

"But somehow you and Zoe—"

"About Zoe," Lauren interrupted. She knew Mitch wasn't thrilled about her and Zoe sleuthing around with the previous murder investigations. Hopefully, the police would solve this one quickly – if it was an ordinary hit and run and Ralph had not been deliberately targeted – and she and Zoe wouldn't have to get involved.

But hadn't she thought exactly the same thing before? She pushed that to one side in her tired brain.

"What about Zoe?" Mitch's gaze narrowed. "She's not in any trouble, is she?'

"Of course not," she reassured him. "It's just that—" why was this so awkward? "—she's wondering if you know anyone else you could set her up with on a blind date."

He chuckled. "She's already shot down two colleagues I thought might be suitable for her."

"She said they were too serious," Lauren replied.

"Okay." He grinned. "I'll see who I can come up with."

"Thank you." Lauren touched his arm.

He gave her a tender kiss goodnight, then walked her up the porch steps.

"Do we have an audience tonight?" he smiled.

"You never know with Zoe and Annie," Lauren replied, flashing back to her first dates with him, and discovering that Zoe and Annie had spied on them through the window overlooking the porch.

"I'll drop by the café tomorrow," he told her, pressing a kiss on her forehead.

She waved goodbye, then entered the cottage.

"Annie? Zoe?" she called out.

"Brrt!" Annie scampered down the hall to greet her.

Lauren picked her up and held her close. "I missed you, too."

"You could have asked Mitch in for a coffee or something." Zoe appeared. "I wouldn't have minded."

"Thanks, but all I want to do is turn in."

"I know the feeling." Zoe nodded. "I'll see you in the morning."

CHAPTER 3

"Save Gold Leaf Valley! Save our senior center!" The chanting reached the interior of the café the next morning.

"What's going on?" Zoe rushed to one of the large windows and looked out. Seniors marched along the street in front of the coffee shop, waving signs.

Lauren joined her cousin. So did Annie.

"Brrt?" Annie looked up at Lauren and then peered through the large glass window.

"I think they're protesting," Lauren told the cat.

"But why are they doing it here?" Zoe asked. "We don't have anything to do with the center closing."

"There's Martha." Lauren gestured to the curly haired woman pushing her walker along the street. She'd tied a sign that read *Save Our Senior Center* to her handlebar.

"I recognize some of the protestors from last night," Zoe said. "Look, there's Denise."

"I wonder if Barry is there as well," Lauren mused, "since Denise is his assistant."

"Is Mrs. Finch there?" Zoe squinted. "I can't see her."

"It might be too much for her. There's Hans." Lauren waved to him through the window. The dapper German waved back to her, a smile on his lips.

"Maybe we should offer them half price lattes while they're outside our shop," Zoe suggested. "They might be getting thirsty. I know we said we'd organize a discount for everyone next week, but—"

"It's a good idea." Lauren smiled.

"Brrt!"

"We could give half price coffees to the seniors outside and anyone who supports them for the next hour," Lauren added.

"Awesome! I'll go and tell them." Zoe grinned.

This morning, business had been slow, so Lauren didn't mind offering a big discount to the protestors. It would keep her and Zoe busy and they'd still make a profit – although a small one – on the lattes.

Annie trotted over to the *Please Wait to be Seated* sign, ready to greet the next customer who entered.

"Come on in!" Zoe held the door open. Hans and a few others walked into the café.

"Brrt?" Annie asked Hans.

"I think we will all sit together today, *Liebchen*." His eyes twinkled as he looked down at her.

Annie looked at the three people crowding behind Hans, as if she were counting them.

"Brrt!" She walked sedately to a table that seated six, situated in the middle of the room.

"Thank you, little one." Hans sat down. Annie hopped onto the spare chair next to him.

"What should we order, hmm?" he asked her.

"We can give you a twenty-five percent discount on the cupcakes,"

Lauren said as she approached. "And half price coffee, hot chocolate, or tea."

"Have you heard about Ralph Lapton?" Hans asked. "It was on the news this morning."

"Yes." Lauren nodded. If Hans had been on his own, she would have told him that she and Zoe had discovered the victim, but she didn't know the other three seniors who were with him, and what their reaction would be to her revelation.

"Brrt!" Annie jumped off the chair and trotted to the *Please Wait to be Seated* sign.

"Hello." Martha peered over the top of her walker. "You must be the cat everyone talks about. You're a cutie."

"Brrt." Annie sounded pleased.

Lauren hurried over to Martha. "Hans and the others are sitting over there." She gestured to the large table in the middle of the room. Would you like to join them?"

"Why are you protesting outside our café?" Zoe had come inside.

"Because it's prime real estate and lots of people will see us." Martha grinned.

"It will bring a lot of attention to our cause."

"I would agree with you," Lauren said, "but I'm afraid we're not very busy this morning."

"I'm sure that will change," Martha told her. "We're going to take turns coming in here and getting a half price latte. That's a good deal."

"Brrt?" Annie looked enquiringly at Martha's rolling walker. She reached up and patted the seat with her paw.

"What's she saying?" Martha asked.

"I think she wants to know if she can have a ride on your walker," Lauren replied.

"Sure thing, cute gal." Martha grinned at the cat. "Hop on!"

Annie jumped on to the padded vinyl seat.

Martha pushed slowly and the two of them trundled to the table where her friends were gathered.

Annie's eyes widened at the rolling motion. "Brrt!" *Look at me!*

Lauren watched Hans make a fuss of the feline as she hopped off the walker and onto the chair next to him.

"I'll get these lattes started if you take Martha's order," she murmured to Zoe.

"Sure thing!" Zoe dashed over to the table.

Lauren watched Zoe laugh with Martha as she scribbled down an order.

"Vanilla cupcake and a large cappuccino." Zoe slapped the note down on the counter. "You didn't make vanilla cupcakes today because Mitch is stopping by, did you?" she teased.

"No." Lauren blushed at the lie. Vanilla was Mitch's favorite.

"Today might turn out to be super busy after all." Zoe eyed the triple chocolate, and lemon poppyseed cupcakes, and Ed's apricot Danishes in the glass case.

"Have you told Ed what happened last night?" Zoe asked.

"No." Lauren shook her head. "You know he doesn't like to be disturbed when he's baking."

"That's for sure." Zoe giggled. "We can tell him about last night later."

"That's if he doesn't hear the commotion outside." The sound of chanting grew louder as more seniors joined the protest.

"More business for us," Zoe said brightly.

The rest of the morning passed in a blur as they made lattes, cappuccinos, and hot chocolate for their elderly customers. To Lauren's disappointment, Mrs. Finch didn't come in.

"Maybe we should visit Mrs. Finch after we close," Zoe suggested during a brief lull. "Make sure she's okay."

"Good idea. I think Annie would like to come as well." Lauren looked over at the cat. Hans had rejoined the protestors, and now Annie nestled in her pink cat bed.

"Ooh, it's Ms. Tobin." Zoe looked up from the latte she was making and waved to the tall, thin woman.

"I'll go." Lauren stepped around the counter and greeted their customer.

"Brrt?" Annie ambled up to Ms. Tobin, looking a little sleepy. Lauren was sure that somehow Annie knew how much Ms. Tobin looked forward to her interaction with her.

"Could you find me a table, Annie?" Ms. Tobin scanned the room. "You seem very busy, Lauren."

"We're running a half price coffee special for the protestors. And their supporters," she added hastily. "Zoe and I saw you at the senior center party last night."

"Yes, I saw you two as well," Ms. Tobin replied. "In fact, I'm going to march with them as soon as I have a latte."

"Then we'll give you fifty percent off your coffee, and I'm also offering a discount on the cupcakes for this morning," Lauren replied, not wanting the older woman to feel left out.

"That's very nice of you," Ms. Tobin replied with a small smile. "Thank you. Oh – I must tell you how delicious your cupcakes were last night. Are you going to make them for the café? I thought the maraschino cherry was an elegant touch."

"It was a new flavor I made for the party," Lauren told her. "But I can definitely make them for our customers."

"Good. I'd love to have another one." Ms. Tobin followed Annie to a small table near the counter.

Lauren watched Annie jump onto the chair opposite Ms. Tobin and "chat" to her for a couple of minutes.

"Should we take her order?" Zoe asked, holding a tray of four cappuccinos. "I've got to deliver this to the table in the back."

"I'll do it," Lauren replied. Until recently, Ms. Tobin had expected table service, although they usually only did that for the elderly and infirm. Ms. Tobin was neither. But she had mellowed recently, and now usually walked over to the counter to order.

"She loved our cupcakes last night," she told Zoe before her cousin threaded her way through the tables.

"Awesome!" Zoe grinned.

"What can I get you, Ms. Tobin?" Lauren asked as she approached the older woman and Annie.

"Brrt," Annie said conversationally, glancing at Lauren.

"I'll have my usual large latte, Lauren. And one of Ed's pastries. But you didn't have to come over here to get my order – I was just about to go over to the counter."

"No problem," Lauren said cheerfully.

"Everyone was so upset last night about Ralph Lapton's announcement," Ms. Tobin continued.

"So were we," Lauren replied.

"Oh, have you heard about him? He was run over!" Disapproval flickered over Ms. Tobin's expression.

"Yes." Lauren nodded. She didn't know whether to tell her regular customers that she and Zoe had found Ralph's body. Perhaps she should talk it over with Zoe first.

"I do hope you and Zoe won't get involved in his death." Ms. Tobin tutted.

For a moment, she sounded like her old prickly self, but Lauren thought it might be from concern.

"I hope so too," Lauren replied diplomatically. And right now, it was the truth.

Lauren filled Ms. Tobin's order, wondering when Mitch would drop by. It might not be until his lunch break, or late in the afternoon. Would he have any news about the hit and run? Had it been an accident? Or had it been ... deliberate?

Lauren shivered as she remembered the disgruntled seniors from last night. Even this morning, in the café, they were talking about what they could do to stop the demolition of the senior center.

Lauren carefully placed Ms. Tobin's latte and cupcake on the table.

"Are you coming to the meeting in the church hall this evening?" Ms. Tobin asked her.

"Yes, Zoe and I will be there."

"Good." Ms. Tobin nodded. "Perhaps we can all come up with some ideas about what to do."

"I hope so."

"Brrt!"

Annie departed back to her bed, settling down for a snooze.

"So good of her to sit with me for a while," Ms. Tobin murmured as she gazed after the silver-gray tabby.

"She must know that you like her to do that," Lauren offered. She hurried back to the counter, noticing a middle-aged couple ready to pay the bill.

At lunch time, Lauren was ready to take a break for the rest of the day – except she couldn't. Zoe's idea of half

price beverages had been successful –
perhaps too much so. But now, the crowd
had thinned out a little in the café, and
also outside on the street. Perhaps some
of the seniors had gone home for lunch?

"Want your lunchbreak first?" Lauren
asked her cousin.

"I'm okay. You go," Zoe replied. "I
can handle things here."

"I'll just tell Ed. He'll help you if you
need him to."

"Go." Zoe shooed her away.

Lauren pushed the swinging kitchen
doors open. Ed stood at the workbench,
working a batch of dough. His short
auburn hair was shaggy, and his arms
looked like monster rolling pins, full of
muscle.

"Have you heard about the senior
center's landlord wanting to pull it down
and build a resort instead?" Lauren asked.

"Yep." Ed glanced up briefly. "And he
was killed last night."

"Zoe and I found the body – well, Zoe
did."

"Ouch." Ed grimaced.

She told him she was taking a quick
lunch break and left him to his dough.

Once inside the cottage, she sank onto a kitchen chair and wiggled her feet. Even wearing sneakers, her feet were tired already today.

Lauren grabbed a quick bowl of granola, promising herself a delicious dinner as a reward. Maybe she and Zoe could grab a burger after the meeting tonight, or order a pizza.

After fifteen minutes, she headed back to the café. She didn't want to leave Zoe on her own for long with so many customers.

Zoe dashed off to the cottage for her own lunch, grabbing a panini as she did so.

Lauren surveyed the customers eating, drinking, and talking to each other. Annie dozed in her cat bed. Everything was under control.

Mitch entered the café, and immediately Lauren's heartbeat went haywire.

"Hi." He strode to the counter.

"Hi," she greeted him. Even after a couple of months of dating, she still felt shy and breathless in his presence.

"I had to walk around the protestors to get in here." He chuckled.

"Apparently, this is prime real estate." She told him about Martha's reasoning for holding the protest outside.

"Are you going to the meeting tonight?"

"Yes. Are you?"

"I have to work late today. But maybe we could have dinner together tomorrow night?"

"Yes." Lauren smiled.

"Good." He stood gazing at her for a moment, his dark brown eyes warm. Clearing his throat as if he suddenly remembered something, he said, "Your car's been checked out and it's in the clear. I've parked it outside your cottage."

"Thank you."

"Because we're seeing each other, I have to recuse myself from the case."

"I understand," Lauren replied. "You don't mind, do you?"

"No." He shook his head. "I'm just glad you're okay."

"Was it an accidental hit and run?" Lauren asked.

"We don't know for sure yet." His face tightened. "The medical examiner is still working on it."

They talked for a few more minutes, then Mitch ordered a large latte.

Lauren ground the coffee beans and steamed the milk, the grinding and hissing soothing to her. She picked up a vanilla cupcake with the tongs and placed it into a brown paper bag for him.

"From me," she said when he looked at her in surprise.

"Thanks." His smile lit up his face.

Zoe came back from her lunch break a few minutes after Mitch had departed.

"What did I miss?" She looked around the café.

Lauren smiled to herself. "I'm seeing Mitch tomorrow night."

"Can you ask him if he can find a gorgeous blind date for me?" Zoe joked.

"I already have," Lauren replied. "Last night. He's going to try."

"You're the best." Zoe beamed at her. "Otherwise, I might take up Martha on her offer to introduce me to someone." Her gaze landed on the string-art picture of a pink frosted cupcake hanging on the wall opposite.

"Going to do more string-art?" Lauren asked.

"I can't decide what to make," Zoe replied. "I've created so many in the last three months – one for you, one for me, one for Annie, one for here, one for Ed, one for Mrs. Finch, Hans, Father Mike, and even Ms. Tobin." She giggled at that. "I might be getting all—"

"Don't say it." Lauren shook her head.

"Maybe I should see if Mrs. Finch has any craft ideas," Zoe mused. "Has she been in yet?"

"No. We should check on her after we close this afternoon."

"It will be tight if we don't want to be late for the meeting, but yes, we should."

The afternoon wasn't as busy, which Lauren was grateful for. At three o'clock, Annie ambled over to the door of the private hallway.

"Brrt," she called to Lauren.

"Do you want to take the rest of the afternoon off?" She stepped around the counter and reached the feline. Only a few tables were occupied right now.

"Brrp," Annie agreed.

"Okay." Lauren smiled as she unlocked the door and watched Annie scamper down the hall and through the cat flap.

"I wish I could go home, too," Zoe joked as Lauren returned to the counter. "Maybe I need a little pick me up."

"You're reading my mind." Lauren ground the beans for two regular mochas. "Maybe we should save a cupcake for each of us."

"Now you're reading *my* mind." Zoe grinned.

Ed poked his head through the kitchen door. "I'm heading home now, Lauren."

"Okay," Lauren replied.

"Are you going to the meeting tonight?" Zoe asked him.

"Maybe," he replied. "Father Mike might be able to come up with an idea to help the seniors."

"We'll be there," Zoe told him.

He nodded, then retreated inside the kitchen.

As soon as Lauren's watch read five o'clock, she locked the front door. Their last customer had departed two minutes ago.

"Let's clean up quickly." Zoe started stacking the wooden chairs onto the tables.

Lauren plugged in the vacuum and ran it around the wooden floorboards. She'd already peeked into the kitchen and Ed had left it sparkling clean. All they had to do was wash the last few dirty cups and plates. Although she had a dishwasher, sometimes it was quicker to do a few dishes by hand.

"I'll take care of the kitchen." Zoe finished stacking the chairs. "And then we can check on Mrs. Finch."

"I'll see if Annie wants to come with us." Lauren finished vacuuming, then dashed through the private hallway to the cottage.

"Brrt?" Annie asked, looking up from lapping at her bowl of water in the kitchen.

"Would you like to quickly visit Mrs. Finch?" Lauren asked.

"Brrt!" *Yes!*

"You'll have to wear your harness." Lauren unhooked the lavender contraption from the kitchen wall.

Annie's mouth settled into a pout, but she allowed Lauren to buckle it on.

Lauren stroked her silver-gray fur, marveling once more at how soft and velvety it felt.

"We'll come home after we see Mrs. Finch, then Zoe and I have to go to a meeting at the church hall," she told the cat. "To see if we can help Mrs. Finch and her friends keep their senior center."

"Brrp," Annie replied, as if she understood.

"Zoe might have finished the dishes by now." She and Annie walked down the private hallway and into the café.

"All done." Zoe came out of the swinging kitchen doors. "Let's go!"

They walked around the block to Mrs. Finch's house.

"I hope she's okay," Lauren said as they neared the sweet, cream painted Victorian house. Mrs. Finch had a small front yard with a neat lawn.

"Me too." Zoe knocked on the door.

"Hello, girls." Mrs. Finch slowly opened the door. "Hello, Annie, dear."

"Brrt!"

"We just wanted to see if you were okay," Lauren said.

"Are you going to the meeting tonight at the church hall?" Zoe asked.

"I don't think so," Mrs. Finch sounded regretful. "I enjoyed last night – until Ralph made his announcement – but I think two evenings out in a row are too much for me right now. I was planning to come to the café today, but …"

"We understand," Lauren replied.

"We're still on for string-art club Friday night, aren't we?" Zoe asked.

"Of course." Mrs. Finch smiled. "I do so enjoy our little get-togethers."

"Awesome!"

"We'd better get going," Lauren said, glancing at her watch, "if we want to get to the meeting on time."

"Of course. And you can tell me all about it tomorrow when I come to the café."

"We will," Zoe assured her.

They waved goodbye to her, and walked back to their cottage. After

Lauren gave Annie her dinner, she and Zoe grabbed their purses and strode to the church hall. It wasn't very far away, and it seemed silly to drive such a short distance.

"Phew!" Zoe remarked. "All this exercise is giving me an appetite!"

"I wouldn't mind going to the diner for a burger afterward," Lauren admitted, "or getting pizza."

"Deal." Zoe grinned. "Either sounds great to me."

They approached the cream painted church. Groups of seniors stood outside, talking to each other.

"There's Hans." Zoe waved to him.

"And Martha." Lauren watched the older woman push her walker into the church hall.

"And a lot of people who were at the protest today," Lauren observed, smiling at them.

"Maybe we should go inside and get a seat," Zoe murmured. "I hope there are enough chairs for everyone – after the day we've had, I don't know if I could stand for another couple of hours."

"I know exactly what you mean," Lauren replied, her feet beginning to ache once more.

They entered the hall. Black folding chairs had been set out in rows, and half the seats were filled already.

"Let's sit at the back," Lauren suggested. "We should still be able to hear well."

"Because some of the others might need to sit up front," Zoe finished the thought. "Good idea."

To their relief, there were plenty of vacant chairs at the rear.

"Hi, Father Mike!" Zoe greeted the priest.

"Hi, girls." He smiled at them, then sobered. "I guess you've heard by now what happened to Mr. Ralph Lapton."

"Mm-hm," Zoe replied. She lowered her voice. "We were the ones who found him."

"My goodness!" His eyes widened. "I'm sorry, I had no idea."

"We haven't told anyone – well, except for—"

"Ed," Zoe finished.

"Do you have any news about his death, Lauren?" Father Mike asked. "Forget I asked," he said a second later, looking embarrassed. "It's just that you're dating Mitch and—"

"No, I'm afraid I don't know anything," Lauren told him.

"Except that we're in the clear," Zoe added. "Well, Lauren's car has been cleared – the police checked it all over."

"Good." Father Mike nodded. "It looks like we've got a large turn-out for tonight." He frowned for an instant. "Eventually, Barry from the senior center will have to contact Ralph's wife and find out what she intends on doing with the property."

"Do you think she'll inherit it?" Lauren asked.

"That's my guess," the priest replied.

"When will we know, do you think?" Zoe asked.

"I have no idea." Father Mike looked regretful. "But in case Crystal does go ahead with the scheme to build a resort, I think we need to come up with a plan."

More people walked into the hall, and Lauren and Zoe left Father Mike to greet them.

"I hope everyone's got some ideas." Zoe stifled a yawn. "Right now, I don't have anything."

"Me either," Lauren said regretfully. She hadn't even had time today to mix up cake batter for the morning.

After a few more minutes, the hall filled up. She spotted Ed in a middle row, talking to another man. Multiple conversations buzzed around her and Zoe, until Father Mike called for quiet. Barry, the director of the senior center, and his assistant Denise, stood on either side of the priest at the front of the room.

After saying a few words about the problem the senior center faced, Father Mike called for ideas.

"Unfortunately, the owner, whoever that is going to be now," Barry said, "is within their rights to not renew our lease. But there are avenues we can explore. For instance, the new owner will need building approval to build this proposed resort. We can object, and make sure it all goes through the proper channels."

"But where will we go if they don't renew the lease?" a man shouted.

"My house is too small for everyone!" a bald man chortled.

"The church can host some activities right here," Father Mike told them. "I'm sure we can arrange movie nights and card games."

"That will be very helpful," Denise told the priest, "and we appreciate the offer. But a lot of people depend on our hot lunch program, and the kitchen here is too small – even if we were able to use it," she added hastily.

"Have sandwiches instead," a large woman called out.

"Lauren and Zoe could make us cupcakes," Martha suggested.

Lauren looked at Zoe with wide eyes. She would welcome the extra business, but how many extra dozen cupcakes would she need to bake each day?

"You can't eat cupcakes every day," another woman scoffed.

"You can't?" Zoe whispered to Lauren. "You can in my world."

Lauren stifled a smile. "Mine too," she whispered back.

"Who killed him?" a man asked.

"We don't have any news as to that," Barry said a trifle pompously. "I'm sure it will be on the front page of the newspaper if the police make an arrest."

More and more suggestions were shouted out, as well as people wondering aloud if the hit and run had been accidental or deliberate.

Father Mike took control of the meeting once more.

"I suggest we make a list of what activities you'd like to continue here, in the hall," he said. "If the worst comes to the worst and your lease isn't renewed."

"Poker!" Martha shouted.

"I'll pass a list around and you can write down what you'd like," Father Mike said.

"Have these young ones got any ideas?" A man with a pot belly stood up and pointed to Lauren and Zoe.

Lauren's face flamed as most of the seniors turned around and stared at them.

"I do." Zoe stood. "Like I suggested last night, you could do a crowdfunding campaign. But instead of raising money to buy the property from whoever owns it now, you could raise cash to buy a block of land and build your own senior center. And no one would be able to take it away from you."

"Yeah!" Martha pointed at Zoe. "I like that idea!"

"Our own senior center," a few people murmured.

"It's certainly an idea," Barry spoke over the others. "And one we can definitely look into. But we'd have to find a suitable block of land that would allow the correct zoning. We'll need to do everything properly and get building permission."

"We can build it ourselves!" the pot-bellied man called out. "We did it before and we can do it again!"

Cheers of "Yeah!" rang out.

Denise, Barry's assistant, called for quiet.

"First, we'll need to find out what's going to happen with our current lease. But we can try crowdfunding to raise the money for our own land, so something like this won't happen to us again. Tomorrow I'll research which site is best to use for raising funds."

"Why don't we have another meeting in a couple of days' time?" Barry proposed. "We can hold it at the senior center since the lease is still current, and Father Mike, you're certainly invited."

"Yeah!" the seniors enthused.

The meeting broke up shortly after.

"I knew you were a zippy gal." Martha wheeled up to Zoe and Lauren. "Good idea."

"Thanks," Zoe replied. "It just popped into my head," she whispered to Lauren.

Lauren nodded, and smiled at Martha, and the others who came up to say goodbye to them. The seniors seemed to be looking forward to the next meeting and told Lauren and Zoe they had to attend.

"Yes, you must be there," Denise said before she left the hall. "I think crowdfunding is a great idea. I just hope we can raise enough money."

"Me too," Zoe said.

"And of course, we'd need to find a vacant block of land," Denise continued. "One that's not too expensive."

"Ooh, if you lose the lease, can you dismantle the center and save all the building materials for your new one?" Zoe's eyes sparkled. "Or does the improved building belong to the owner, even though you provided some of the supplies?"

"That's a very interesting point," Denise replied thoughtfully. "We'll have to look into that."

Lauren and Zoe made their way out of the church hall, waving goodbye to everyone.

"We'll have to catch up with Hans when he comes into the café," Zoe told Lauren.

"Definitely," she agreed.

Lauren's stomach growled by the time they reached Gary's Burger Diner.

"I'm starving!" Zoe opened the door with a whoosh and they walked into the stainless steel and glass interior.

"There's Cindy." Lauren waved to the waitress at the hostess station.

"Hi, guys." Cindy greeted them with a smile. Her long blonde hair was swept back with violet barrettes. "Are you dining in or taking out?"

"In," Lauren and Zoe chorused.

"Take your pick." Cindy gestured to the half-empty restaurant as she handed them menus.

They chose a two-seater in the middle of the room.

"I don't see many people here from the meeting," Zoe said as she studied the other diners.

A family of six occupied a large table, while a few middle-aged couples laughed and chatted as they ate huge burgers.

"Maybe they had their dinner before the meeting," Lauren suggested. She didn't need to look at the menu – she couldn't wait to taste a smoky barbecue special.

"Early bird special." Zoe grinned. "It's a shame they don't have that for people our age."

Cindy came over to take their order.

"I bet I know what you guys would like." Cindy smiled at them, her notepad ready.

"You probably do," Lauren said with a rueful smile.

Zoe glanced at Lauren. They nodded at the same time.

"Yep, we'll have the usual please," Zoe declared.

"Coming right up." Cindy winked at them before hurrying to the kitchen.

They didn't have to wait long before they received their meals. Lauren's plate was filled to the brim with golden fries, and a large burger. The juicy-looking meat patty hung over the edge of the bun, and fronds of crisp lettuce and slices of fresh tomato peeked out. The aroma of smoky barbecue sauce teased Lauren's appetite. A chocolate shake finished off the meal.

Zoe's order was identical.

"I just love this burger." Zoe sighed after she enjoyed her first bite.

"Mm-hm," Lauren mumbled around a mouthful of flavorsome beef.

Soft folk rock music played in the background as they concentrated on eating until Lauren finally pushed her plate away. A few fries and a little bit of burger bun remained on her plate.

"I think I'm stuffed." Zoe patted her slim stomach. She'd eaten everything on her plate. She slurped up the last of the chocolate shake. "Now I'm good to go."

"Me too."

After paying, they turned to leave. The door swung open and Crystal walked in, furtively looking around as if to check nobody recognized her. She wore a tawny messy bun beanie with her distinctive strawberry-blonde locks poking out at the top, and large black sunglasses shielding her eyes.

Zoe drew in her breath.

Lauren watched Crystal hurry over to a small table in the rear, her faded denim jeans and white sweatshirt a total contrast to the gown she'd worn last night at the senior center party.

"Let's say hello to her." Zoe nudged Lauren.

Zoe zipped over to the widow. Lauren followed, wondering if they should disturb Crystal.

"Hi." Zoe smiled at her.

"Oh – hi," Crystal said with less enthusiasm. She took off her sunglasses and narrowed her green eyes, her expression clearing. "You were there last night. Cupcakes and coffee."

"That's us," Lauren admitted. "Are we intruding?" She didn't know whether she wanted Crystal to say yes or no.

Crystal shrugged. Zoe took it as an invitation to sit down at the table, eyeing the spare chair at the next table and then glancing at Lauren.

Lauren took the hint and dragged the stainless-steel chair over and sat down.

"You've caught me," Crystal said in a low voice.

Lauren and Zoe looked at each other. Was Crystal going to confess to something?

"I've had a craving all day for these burgers," Crystal continued.

"Do you live around here?" Zoe asked. "I haven't seen you or your husband before last night."

"We live – lived – in Sacramento, but we have a cabin nearby for getaways. That's how I know how good the burgers are."

"We're sorry about your husband," Lauren said.

"Thanks." A not-quite smile touched Crystal's lips. She stared at them for a moment. "The police said he was found by two women—"

"Guilty," Zoe admitted.

"Huh." Crystal sank back in her chair. "It really is a small world."

"And this is a small town." Lauren gave a tentative smile.

"How did you get home last night?" Zoe asked curiously. "You left before your husband did." She seemed to ignore Lauren's admonishing frown.

"I called a cab," Crystal replied. "It wasn't the first time I've left without him." She shook her head. "There's no point trying to reason with him when he's like that. So I waited in the foyer for the cab to arrive."

"Did you go back to Sacramento?" Lauren asked, despite herself. "Or to your cabin?"

"The house in Sacramento," Crystal replied. "But this morning – when the police notified me—" she shuddered. "I just couldn't face the neighbors today, so I drove to the cabin as soon as I could." She hesitated. "I know your seniors were unhappy about his announcement last night, but they're not the first who have felt like that. Our Sacramento neighbors are mad at him because he exceeded the building height on the barn he erected."

"A barn in Sacramento?" Lauren frowned.

"He wanted a man cave." Crystal sighed. "When he gets an idea – got, I mean – in his head, there was no stopping him."

"What happened to the barn?" Zoe asked.

"He was supposed to amend it and take off the top part, but he hadn't yet. The deadline was next week. The neighbors might have taken care of it by the time I go back there."

"They hated it that much?" Lauren said.

"Yeah."

There was a short silence.

"We went ahead with the meeting tonight," Lauren remarked. "I hope that wasn't inappropriate."

"Oh, right. I totally forgot about that after – after …" She blinked fiercely. "You guys do what you need to do."

After an awkward moment, Lauren and Zoe told her briefly about the gathering at the church hall.

"Do you know what you'll do with the senior center?" Zoe probed.

"Zoe!" Lauren whispered.

Crystal gave a short laugh. "Well, first I'll have to see if I inherit."

"You don't know?" Zoe's expression was skeptical.

Crystal scanned the room, as if checking for eavesdroppers, then leaned toward them. "I got the feeling lately that Ralph was thinking of looking around for a new wife."

"No way!" Zoe's mouth parted.

"I'm sorry," Lauren offered.

"We've been married four years. I know I'm a trophy wife. But I was okay with that. We didn't discuss money or wills, or any of that stuff. I didn't even know what he intended to do with the senior center until we were on our way there last night."

"Oh," Lauren replied.

"Why did you marry him?" Zoe asked inquisitively. Lauren nudged her.

"Because he could be very charming when he wanted something," Crystal told them. "And back then, he wanted me. I told myself marrying him was better than working for minimum wage. I was twenty-eight. I was fond of him – then. He said I could do whatever I wanted within reason, and he'd give me a generous monthly allowance that I could spend on whatever I liked. I thought it was a good deal, so I took it."

"But now?" Zoe asked eagerly.

"But now …" Crystal shrugged. "I don't know how I feel. Even though our marriage wasn't great right now, he was still my husband. And until I see his lawyer, I don't know if I'll be penniless or wealthy."

Cindy came over to take Crystal's order. Lauren and Zoe excused themselves, and left the diner.

"Wow," Zoe murmured as they walked home. "I feel sorry for her."

"Me too," Lauren replied.

"I hope Ralph provided for her in the will," Zoe continued.

"Definitely," Lauren replied, then halted mid-step. She stared at Zoe.

"Crystal didn't say if she'd signed a pre-nup."

CHAPTER 4

"You're a genius!" Zoe blinked at Lauren. "Yeah, if she had a bad pre-nup and she knew he was looking around for wife number two – or three or four—"

"Because Crystal mightn't have been his first wife."

"Then she might have run over him herself! So she wouldn't be broke and homeless when he divorced her. If she doesn't inherit anything, she could contest the will."

"But we don't know yet if his death was deliberate, or an accident," Lauren pointed out.

"But we might tomorrow." Zoe grinned. "When you ask Mitch."

The two of them continued to speculate on the short walk home.

"Brrt?" Annie greeted them in the hall when Lauren and Zoe entered the cottage. A furry toy hedgehog dangled from her mouth.

"I'm sorry," Lauren told the feline. "I didn't get you a burger tonight."

"You've already had your dinner," Zoe pointed out.

"Brrt." Annie's lower lip stuck out, the hedgehog at a precarious angle.

"Mrs. Finch is coming to the café tomorrow," Lauren tried to cheer her up.

"Brrp?" Annie looked at them enquiringly.

"That's right," Zoe added. "And you can tell her about everything you did today."

Annie looked mollified as she strolled to the living room.

"I hope we're forgiven," Lauren said as she followed the cat. Mrs. Finch was one of Annie's favorites, and Annie usually stayed with the elderly lady the whole time she was at the café, communicating with her usual "brrts" and "brrps" as Mrs. Finch told Annie her news.

"Me, too."

Lauren and Zoe went to bed. Annie hopped up on Lauren's bed, turned around in a circle, and settled down for the night. Lauren smiled as she stroked the silver-gray tabby's soft fur. She must be forgiven.

***

The next day, Mrs. Finch was one of their first customers.

Annie ran to greet her, choosing a small table near the counter.

"No protestors yet," Lauren said, as she approached the duo. She quickly told Mrs. Finch about yesterday's protest outside the café.

Zoe joined her. "Don't forgot to tell her we bumped into Crystal last night."

"The new landlord's wife?" Mrs. Finch looked interested.

Zoe related the story while Lauren made a latte and plated a vanilla cupcake. It had been a bit of a rush job this morning to make the batter and bake the cupcakes before they opened, but she and Zoe had managed it. And right now, Ed was proving his second batch of dough in the kitchen.

"And she said she caught a taxi back to Sacramento," Zoe related to Mrs. Finch as Lauren returned to the table with the order.

"My goodness," Mrs. Finch exclaimed.

"It must have cost a fortune," Lauren added as she set the coffee down in front of Mrs. Finch.

"It sounds as if the police will be able to verify that," Mrs. Finch said as she picked up her cup with wobbly hands.

"She must know they would check up on something like that," Zoe mused. "So I guess she must be telling the truth."

"Probably," Lauren agreed. She'd learnt this past year that sometimes what sounded like the truth could be a lie – or something that just skirted the edge of veracity.

"Brrt!" Annie's ears pricked up and she jumped off the chair next to Mrs. Finch's. She scampered to the *Please Wait to be Seated* sign.

Lauren turned. "Hi, Hans."

"Hello, Lauren, and Zoe. Hello, *Liebchen*." He bent stiffly to stroke Annie.

"Hi, Hans." Zoe waved to him from Mrs. Finch's table.

"Where should I sit today, Annie?" he asked.

"Brrt!" she said importantly, leading him to Mrs. Finch's table.

"You want me to sit here?" He smiled at the elderly lady.

"Please do, Hans," Mrs. Finch told him. "If Annie wants you to join me, she must have a reason."

"That is true." He sank down on the vacant chair. "But where will you sit, hmm, Annie?"

"Brrt!" Annie jumped on a neighboring chair, then looked appealingly at Lauren.

"You want me to bring the chair over to Mrs. Finch and Hans?" Lauren couldn't help smiling.

"Brrp," Annie replied. *Yes.*

"Okay."

Annie hopped off the chair so Lauren could pick it up and carry it the short distance.

"There is plenty of room, *Liebchen.*" Hans indicated the side of the small table.

"Brrt." Annie jumped onto the chair again and surveyed Mrs. Finch and Hans, looking pleased with herself.

"Maybe Annie wants Hans to fill in Mrs. Finch about the meeting last night," Zoe suggested.

"Brrt!"

"What can we get you, Hans?" Lauren asked.

"A cappuccino, please. And one of Ed's pastries if they are ready."

"The first batch are. Blueberry Danish."

"That sounds wonderful." Hans smiled at Lauren and Zoe.

"We'll leave you three to it." Zoe grinned as she accompanied Lauren back to the counter.

From her vantage point, Lauren heard Annie "converse" with Mrs. Finch and Hans by a series of "Brrts" and "Brrps" while Hans told Mrs. Finch about the church hall meeting last evening.

"Now Annie will know all about the meeting as well." Zoe giggled.

More customers trickled in before lunch but there was still no sign of any protestors. Hans and Mrs. Finch departed, Hans telling them he would accompany Mrs. Finch home.

"Brrt," Annie sound approving as she watched them stroll out of the café.

"Now you know as much as we do about what's happening with the senior center," Zoe joked to the cat.

"Brrp." Annie ambled to her cat bed, turned around, and sank down into its cushiony depths.

"I wish I was a cat." Zoe sighed.

"Me too," Lauren told her.

A short while later, Annie woke up from her snooze, her ears pricking. She padded to the door that led to the private hallway of the cottage.

"Would you like to take a break?" Lauren headed over to her.

"Brrt!"

"There you go." Lauren unlocked the door. "I'll be coming into the cottage for lunch soon."

"Brrp," Annie replied absently, as if she were thinking of something else. She ran down the hall and pushed her way through the cat flap.

Lauren and Zoe served a few more customers before Ed poked his head through the swinging kitchen doors.

"Lauren," he said gruffly, "I need you to come in here for a minute."

Lauren looked at Zoe, mystified. "Okay," she replied.

When she entered the kitchen, her eyes widened. "Annie, what are you doing in here?"

"Brrt!" Annie said proudly, turning around so Lauren could see behind her.

A small brown tabby kitten mewled softly.

"I know animals aren't allowed in here." Ed picked up the scrap of fluff and cradled the creature. "But Annie was making a noise right outside the back door. I opened it and there she was, with this little—" he checked the sex "—girl."

"Mew!" the kitten cried. Her fur was fawn with dark brown stripes. In the middle of her forehead was more dark brown fur in the shape of an M.

"How old do you think she is?" Lauren asked softly.

Ed shrugged. "Not sure, but maybe about six or eight weeks?" He frowned. "She might be the runt of the litter."

"How do you know so much?" Lauren asked curiously.

"My grandmother. She fostered cats for years." He cracked a smile. "I'm going to call her AJ – April Junior. She looks just like a cat Grandma had when I was young – and her name was April."

"Where did you find her, Annie?" Lauren asked.

Annie pawed at the back door. Lauren opened it and Annie led her to the small herb garden. Lauren followed the feline to a bush near the waist high white picket fence – the boundary between the café backyard and her cottage.

"Here?"

"Brrt." Annie tapped her paw on the grass beneath the bush.

"You are so clever." Lauren stroked her. "Is that why you wanted to take a break? You must have come out here through the cat flap in the cottage's back door."

"Brrt." *That's right.*

"Did you know there's a kitten in the kitchen?" Zoe called out. She stood near the herb garden.

Lauren and Annie headed over to her, Lauren filling her in on what happened.

"Oh, lucky Ed." Zoe's brown eyes softened. "A kitten to look after. It's Annie's lost and found at work again!"

"We'll have to check if anyone is looking for her – AJ," Lauren amended.

"He's named her already?"

"Yes."

"He's in trouble," Zoe said.

They returned to the café kitchen, Lauren feeling guilty allowing Annie to come in as well. She was allowed on the café floor with the customers but because of health regulations, she wasn't permitted to be inside the actual kitchen.

Zoe made a fuss over the kitten Ed held, patting it and talking in baby tones to it. Lauren and Annie looked at each other as if both of them were trying to stifle a smile.

"Watch out Ed, or Zoe might catnap her," Lauren joked.

"Nuh-uh." Ed shook his shaggy head. "AJ is all mine."

"We'll have to check the lost and found section of the local newspaper," Lauren said. "And inquire at the vet's. Just in case someone is looking for AJ."

"Yeah, I guess," Ed replied reluctantly.

"She is so adorable." Zoe sighed. Her glance settled on Lauren – and then

Annie. "But you're the most adorable one ever, aren't you, Annie?"

"Brrt!" She looked as if she nodded.

"I guess we'd better get back to work," Lauren said. "The customers will be wondering where we are."

"There were only three when I went to find you," Zoe said. "I'm sure they'll understand."

"I'm going to take AJ home," Ed said. "Get her settled in, and then come straight back."

"No worries." Lauren smiled at him. "She's lucky to have you to look after her."

He nodded, then still cradling the kitten, departed the kitchen.

"Wow," Zoe said softly. "Even if I'd wanted to, I wouldn't have had a chance getting the kitten away from Ed."

"Maybe they're meant to be," Lauren mused, as she gazed fondly at Annie. "Just like Annie and I are – and you, of course."

"Yep, I'm like the fun aunt." Zoe grinned.

"Annie, you'd better go back to the cottage through the back garden," Lauren lowered her voice. "So no one will know you were in here."

"Brrt," Annie replied. Lauren opened the rear door and Annie walked sedately toward the cottage, her plumy silver tail waving in the air.

"I wonder if Ed will actually come back today?" Zoe posed the question.

"I'm sure he will." Lauren checked her watch. "Would you like to grab lunch first?"

"Okay," Zoe agreed. "Do you want me to feed Annie?"

"That would be great. There's beef in gravy in the fridge for her."

"I won't be long," Zoe promised.

Lauren stepped into the dining area and surveyed the room. Her cousin had been correct – only three customers. None of them looked like they needed assistance. She sat down on the stool behind the counter, her thoughts drifting to the little kitten AJ, and Ed's reaction. She hadn't known he was a cat person.

"Hi." Mitch stood at the *Please Wait to be Seated* sign. He wore charcoal slacks and a pale blue dress shirt.

"Oh – hi." She stood up, flustered. She'd been thinking so hard that she hadn't even noticed him enter. Surely that was a first?

"Where's Annie?"

"Taking a break." She came around the counter to greet him.

"Are we still on for tonight?" he asked. "I thought we could go to the bistro."

"Sounds great." She led the way to the counter. "What can I get you?"

He leaned over it. "You," he said softly.

Her cheeks heated, and she caught her breath.

"But I guess right now I'll settle for a large latte and one of your vanilla cupcakes." He smiled.

"Coming right up." She ground the beans, her pulse racing. Usually Mitch was pretty businesslike when he visited her at the café.

"I've got some news," he said as she steamed the milk, the wand hissing.

"What's that?"

He looked around the café but the three customers weren't sitting near them and looked absorbed in eating and drinking.

"It was a deliberate hit and run. They're going off the time of death as the time on his smashed watch."

Her eyes widened. "I thought you were off the case."

"I am, but it's general knowledge at the station," he explained.

She poured the milk into the cardboard cup, taking the time to make a swan design on the surface.

"So it is murder then."

"Yeah." He didn't sound happy. "The car tires were slashed as well."

Lauren took a second to process that, then told him how she and Zoe had run into Crystal the previous evening. "Does she have an alibi for the time of the murder if she caught a cab?"

"Yes. She's already been interviewed and the cab driver confirmed her story. It's all there in the cab records, anyway. He was pretty happy because she gave him a large tip."

Lauren was glad Crystal hadn't lied to them. She'd felt sorry for the other woman. What would it be like to be married to someone you didn't love? She knew if she ever got married, it would be for love, nothing else.

Peeking at Mitch from under her lashes, she wondered if one day Mitch would be the one. *It's too soon to go there.*

"Hey," Mitch said softly. "Where did you go?"

Lauren blinked. "Oh, sorry." She couldn't tell him what she'd been daydreaming about – could she?

Grabbing a vanilla cupcake, she placed it into a paper bag, and popped the lid on his latte.

"I'll pick you at seven." He smiled at her.

"I'll be ready," she promised.

His phone rang. With a grimace he answered it, and mouthed "Work" to her. He nodded goodbye as he strode out of the café.

Lauren gazed after him.

"Mitch?" Zoe appeared next to her.

"Yep."

"Lucky you. Do you want to take your lunch break now?"

"Okay." Lauren grabbed a panini and made her way to the cottage.

"Brrt?" Annie wandered into the homey kitchen.

"Did you eat your lunch?" Lauren looked down at the cat's bowl. A faint smear of gravy decorated it.

"Brrt!" *Yes.*

"Good." Lauren unwrapped her turkey and cranberry sandwich. "Ed's taken AJ home but he's coming back to finish his shift."

"Brrp." Annie jumped onto the chair next to Lauren. She nudged her arm to see what she was eating.

"Want a bit of turkey?" Lauren broke off a small piece of the meat that didn't have any cranberry sauce on it. "Not too much."

Annie delicately took it from her fingers and munched on it.

"I'm going out with Mitch tonight," she reminded the feline, "but Zoe will be here with you."

Annie nudged her arm again, but this time Lauren took it to mean that she understood. When Lauren had finished her quick meal, Annie trotted off to the living room.

"I'll see you afterward." Lauren paused and stood in the doorway. "What are you doing?"

Annie batted a spool under the blue sofa. She repeated the action with another one, this time with red thread wound on it.

"Ohh." Lauren clapped a hand to her mouth. "Those are Zoe's string-art threads."

"Brrt." *Yes.* Annie continued to push the spools under the sofa.

"Where did you get them from? Did you go into Zoe's room?"

"Brrp." *Not telling.*

"Are you playing a game with her?" Lauren tried not to laugh. "I'll see you later."

Still chuckling over Annie's antics, Lauren headed back to the café.

"Ed's back," Zoe told her as she made a cappuccino.

Lauren hurried into the commercial kitchen.

"How's AJ?" she asked.

Ed looked up from spooning blueberries onto pastry rounds. "She's settled in already. I found a cardboard box and lined it with newspapers and some old towels – clean ones – and she was out like a light." He smiled. "I've bought her some kitten food as well."

"That's great," Lauren replied.

"Tomorrow I'll ask at the vet's and read the lost and found column in the newspaper." He frowned. "But if someone does try to claim AJ, I'll definitely be checking them out and making sure they can give her a good home."

"Of course." She left him to his pastry and returned to the café floor.

A few more customers had arrived, and Lauren had no time to tell Zoe about the hide and seek game Annie was playing. In fact, it soon slipped her mind completely.

"Hi, Lauren, and Zoe." Around three o'clock, Denise from the senior center approached the counter. "I was lucky enough to get a parking spot right outside."

Lauren looked through the large plate glass window and saw a shiny blue compact car. It looked familiar.

Denise looked around the room. "Where's Annie?"

"Taking the afternoon off," Lauren replied, switching her attention back to the other woman. She'd planned to check on Annie to see if she wanted to come back to work or stay at home, but they'd been busy since lunch.

"Oh, what a shame. Maybe next time she'll be here."

"Probably," Lauren replied with a smile.

"What can we get you?" Zoe asked. "I can make you a latte with a peacock design on it."

"That sounds interesting."

"How's the crowdfunding research coming along?" Lauren asked.

"There are several different sites." Denise sounded a little frustrated. "And they all take different amounts of commission. If we do go down this route, I want to make sure Barry and I make the best decision for our members."

"Of course," Zoe replied as she steamed the milk.

"Would you like a cupcake or pastry?" Lauren asked.

"I wasn't going to have anything to eat," Denise admitted. She gazed at the glass counter where vanilla, raspberry swirl, and blueberry cupcakes displayed their temptations. "But they look so pretty."

"Thank you." Lauren smiled.

"I'll have vanilla."

"Coming right up." Lauren plated the cupcake.

"Sit anywhere you like." Zoe waved a hand in the direction of the tables as she finished off the peacock design on the latte.

Denise leaned over the counter toward them.

"Do you have an update on the … accident?" she asked in a low tone.

Lauren hesitated. Mitch hadn't told her not to say anything and she knew if he'd given her confidential information earlier, he would have.

"It looks like it was deliberate," she told Denise.

"You didn't tell me that," Zoe scolded.

"Sorry – there hasn't been time."
Lauren gestured to the half-full café.

Zoe nodded.

"So someone ran Ralph over – on purpose." Denise sounded shocked. "How dreadful." She pursed her lips. "I don't know what this world is coming to. His behavior wasn't the best at our party, but that's no reason to kill someone. Is it?" She looked at Lauren and Zoe as if expecting an answer.

"Definitely not," Lauren replied.

"Nope."

"Let us help you with your order," Lauren said, placing the coffee and cake on a tray. "I can bring it to your table.'"

"Thank you." Denise led the way to a small table in the middle of the room. "This should do nicely. Are you two coming to the meeting at the center tomorrow?"

"Yes," Lauren replied. She knew Zoe wouldn't want to miss it.

"Wonderful. I'm sure you two can come up with some more notions in case the new heir – whether it's Ralph's wife

Crystal or someone else – is of the same mind and won't renew our lease."

Not too much pressure then.

Lauren related the conversation to Zoe as they took a few minutes to flop on the stools behind the counter.

"Maybe *we* should run a senior center." Zoe's brown eyes sparkled. "Since they keep asking us for ideas."

"Oh – remember the dusty blue car we saw in the parking lot at the senior center the night of the party?" Lauren made sure to keep her voice low.

"What about it?" Zoe screwed up her face in concentration.

"I think it's Denise's car. Except now it's all washed and shiny."

"No way!" Zoe stared at Lauren. "Where is it?'

"Right outside."

Zoe jumped off the stool and sauntered nonchalantly to the window. She peered out.

"OMG!" she whispered when she got back to the counter. "Do you think she ran over Ralph and that's why she washed her car? So she wouldn't be a suspect?"

"If she did, then why did she park her car right outside?" Lauren furrowed her brow.

"Because she subconsciously wants to show off?"

"Shh – we don't want anyone overhearing." Lauren slanted her cousin a warning look.

At five o'clock, Lauren was more than ready to close up. All she wanted to do was relax under a hot shower, and have dinner with Mitch.

Ed had already left for the day, saying he wanted to check on AJ.

"And then there were two." Zoe joked as Lauren locked the front door.

Lauren quickly filled her in on her conversation with Mitch earlier that day, and the fact that Ralph Lapton's tires had been slashed. As she did so, she realized she'd forgotten to tell Denise about that part.

"I shouldn't be late home tonight," Lauren told her. "Mitch and I have both got early starts tomorrow."

"That's the only thing I don't like about working here." Zoe smiled so

Lauren knew she was teasing. "Getting up at the crack of dawn."

"I think Annie's the only one who enjoys that." The Norwegian Forest Cat usually woke up Lauren in the morning by nudging her, or sometimes licking her cheek.

They made quick work of cleaning the café.

"I still can't quite decide what to make next with my string-art," Zoe said as they trooped to the cottage. "Maybe inspiration will strike tonight, when Annie and I watch TV. I could get started on it tomorrow, maybe."

Annie's antics in hiding Zoe's spools of thread arose in Lauren's mind. But if Annie and Zoe were playing a game, she didn't want to spoil it for either one of them.

Lauren hurried to take a shower, wondering what to wear. She finally settled on her plum wrap dress that Zoe said brought out the natural golden highlights in her light brown hair and her hazel eyes. She finished off the outfit with black kitten heels.

"Have fun!" Zoe called out from the living room.

"I will."

The doorbell rang and Lauren answered it.

Mitch stood in the doorway wearing onyx slacks and a navy dress shirt, under a matching charcoal jacket.

"I'm ready," she said, a little breathless as she admired his appearance.

"Then let's go." He took her hand as they walked down the porch steps.

They drove to the outskirts of Gold Leaf Valley were the restaurant was located. Lauren enjoyed her new favorite dish of pork with four varieties of apples, while Mitch ordered steak with mushroom sauce.

Lauren told him about Annie finding the kitten, and how Ed had transformed into a cat man before their eyes.

"I hope nobody claims AJ," she finished. "I don't want Ed to be disappointed if he has to give her up."

"You've got a good heart." Mitch clasped her hand. His thumb stroked hers.

Electricity raced up her arm.

After they finished their meal, they left the restaurant.

"What about dinner and a movie on Saturday night?" Mitch asked as he held open the car door for Lauren. "We could go to the theater at Zeke's Ridge."

"I'd like that," she told him.

"I'd suggest Friday night but I know it's your knitting club evening." His eyes crinkled in the corners as he smiled. "What exactly do you do there, anyway?"

"Knit," she replied. "Or in Zoe's case, string-art at the moment. And we have coffee – and chat."

"I'm sure Mrs. Finch enjoys you coming over to her house." He started the engine.

"I'm not sure if she prefers our company or Annie's," she joked, but thought the elderly woman liked *all* of them coming to visit her.

Mitch drove her home. "I'm working on finding another blind date for Zoe," he told her as they walked up the porch steps. "My friend's been overseas for a while, but he's just gotten back. I'll see if he's interested."

"Thank you." Lauren reached up on tiptoes and kissed his cheek.

He wrapped his arms around her and kissed her tenderly. "Until Saturday," he murmured.

CHAPTER 5

"Lauren, I can't find my string-art threads." Zoe placed her hands on her hips and surveyed the kitchen.

It was the next morning and Lauren had been crunching her breakfast granola before getting ready to open the café.

"You can't?" She glanced down at Annie, who was licking up the last bit of gravy from her bowl.

Annie looked up at Lauren, her green eyes impossibly wide –and innocent.

"Have you decided which design to make next?" Lauren asked.

"Not yet." Zoe frowned. "But I was going to get all the different colored threads out. I thought going through them and seeing what I've got might give me some inspiration."

"Ah." Lauren didn't know if she was supposed to give the game away. It was obvious that Zoe didn't know about it.

"Have you checked the living room?" she asked.

"Brrt!"

"Yes, but I'd better check it again."
Zoe zoomed to the living room. "I've
already looked in my bedroom."

Lauren heard her from the next room.

"They're not here. Someone's stolen
my string-art threads!"

"Brrt!" *I did!* Annie jumped up on the
chair next to Lauren's.

"I know you did," Lauren whispered to
the cat, "But I thought Zoe was playing
this game with you."

"Brrp." Annie moved her neck so that
it looked like a slight shake of her head.

"Why did you do it?" Lauren asked.

"Brrp." Annie passed a paw over her
ear. A second later, she did it again.

"Ohhh." Understanding dawned. "I
feel the same way, but string-art might be
important to Zoe."

"Brrt." Annie's mouth settled into a
pout.

Lauren stroked the silver-gray tabby.

"Have you looked under the sofa?" she
called out.

"Why would they be under there?" Zoe
sounded exasperated.

A few seconds later, Lauren heard a
muffled, "Found them!"

"Brrp." Annie sounded disappointed.

"Look!" Zoe ran into the kitchen, holding the red, yellow, green, and turquoise spools of thread. "Why were they under the couch?"

"Don't look at me." Lauren tried hard to stifle her smile.

"Annie?" Zoe's eyes rounded, just as Annie's had before when she looked so innocent. "Did you put them there?"

"Brrt!" Annie stood up straight on the chair and thrust out her chest and chin. *Yes, I did!*

"But why?" Zoe frowned.

Annie glanced at Lauren, then jumped off the chair and ran into the living room.

"I think she wants you to follow her," Lauren told her cousin.

"Are you coming?"

"Definitely."

They found Annie in Zoe's bedroom, pawing at the closed closet.

"Is there something in here?" Zoe opened the door.

"Brrt!" Annie pounced on the hammer that Lauren had lent Zoe. Next to the hammer was a clear plastic bag full of shiny silver nails.

Then she passed her paw over her ear.

Zoe stared at Annie and then her string-art tools, a quizzical look on her face.

"I think," Lauren said gently, "Annie is trying to tell you that banging the nails into your canvas makes a lot of noise."

"But why did she steal my threads?" Zoe asked. "They don't make any noise when I string them along the nails to make a picture."

"Maybe she couldn't get into your closet to relocate the hammer or the nails," Lauren suggested. "The hammer might be too heavy for her to move."

"Good point." Zoe nodded. She faced both of them. "I'm sorry. I know I'm a bit noisy at times, but I really enjoyed the whole string-art process at first." She sighed. "To tell you the truth, I was starting to get a bit bored with it. I made a lot of pictures, though."

"You definitely did." Lauren smiled. "Like the goldfish picture you made Annie that's hanging in the living room."

"Brrt!"

"Next time, tell me if I'm being too noisy – with anything."

"We will."

"Brrt!" Annie nudged Zoe's hand, as if to say sorry.

"And you can tell me if I'm being too noisy," Lauren countered.

"I don't think that will ever happen." Zoe laughed. "You're such a quiet person." She looked down. "So are you, Annie. And you're both awesome! I'm so lucky living with both of you."

"Brrt!" *We're all lucky!*

***

Because of the string-art hide and seek, Lauren and Zoe were a few minutes late opening the café that morning. Not that anybody seemed to mind – there weren't any customers lined up outside. Lauren heard the faint rattle of pastry trays as Ed worked in the kitchen.

"I want to get an update on AJ." Zoe bounced into the kitchen.

Lauren followed her. "I'll tell you what we find out," she told Annie.

Annie curled up in her cat bed, watching both of them enter through the swinging doors.

"Have you checked the lost and found column?" Zoe asked Ed.

"This morning," he replied, his hands deep in the pastry he kneaded.

"And?"

"No one's posted about AJ yet," he replied. "I'll go to the vet's after I finish here this afternoon and check."

"I hope no one claims her," Zoe said. "Maybe we could have a bring your pet to work day." She looked at Lauren. "What do you say, boss?"

"I say we need to abide by the health regulations," Lauren replied.

"What about the café area, where Annie is?" Zoe suggested. "Annie could train AJ as her assistant!"

"AJ's only a baby right now," Ed informed her as he pounded the dough. "And she needs to gain some strength first. She mightn't even be a people person like Annie is."

"And we'd have to check with Annie," Lauren added. "She might prefer to be the only cat in the café. But I'm sure she'd like to be friends with AJ."

"We could arrange a playdate." Zoe was not about to be put off.

"Maybe," Ed replied. "When AJ's bigger."

"Just let me know." Zoe beamed.

They left Ed to his work.

"I think I've got kitten cuteness," Zoe confessed when they sat behind the counter.

"I understand." Lauren patted her cousin's shoulder.

"Brrt?" Annie sat up in her basket.

"We're just waiting for our first customer," Zoe said to her. "Ed's going to check at the vet's today about AJ, but he says she's doing well."

Annie's nose wrinkled at the word "vet".

The door opened and a tall, athletic woman pushing a stroller walked in.

"Hi, Claire. Hi, Molly." Lauren smiled at the duo.

"Annie!" The blonde toddler waved to the cat.

"Brrt!" Annie jumped down from her bed and ran over to the little girl.

"I really need a latte," Claire told them. "I know it's just after nine-thirty, but it's been one thing after another this morning already!"

"I know the feeling," Lauren said ruefully.

"Table, pwease, Annie." Molly beamed at the cat.

"Brrt!" *Right this way.*

Claire followed Annie to a four-seater near the counter.

"What would you like?" Lauren asked as she approached, notepad in hand. Zoe accompanied her.

"Wait until you hear about the kitten Annie found yesterday," Zoe enthused. "She is so cute! And small."

"Annie found her in the garden," Lauren put in. "Let me make your order while Zoe tells you all about it." She could see Zoe was bursting to do just that.

"A large latte and one of your delicious cupcakes, please. You choose which one – unless it's triple chocolate," Claire replied.

"Yes, we've got triple chocolate today." Lauren smiled.

"Great! And Molly would like her usual babycino. Isn't that right, darling?"

"Cino, cino!" Molly grinned.

"Coming right up," Lauren promised.

She hurried back to the counter, Zoe's voice in the background as she began telling Claire and Molly about AJ, Annie interjecting with an occasional "Brrt."

Lauren finished off the large latte with a peacock design on the microfoam and carried the order over on a tray.

"Yum, yum." Molly smacked her lips in anticipation as she gently petted Annie using "fairy pats". She pointed to the little white cup with steamed milk froth, a pink and a white marshmallow, and lots of chocolate powder on top. "Ook, Annie."

"Brrp?" Annie asked Lauren.

"Chocolate powder isn't good for you," Lauren told her.

"Brrt." Annie's mouth settled into a pout for a second.

"It looks wonderful." Claire eyed the cupcake with chocolate ganache frosting. "I've told everyone I know about your delicious cupcakes and coffee. And Annie, of course."

Claire and her husband had recently moved from Los Angeles to Gold Leaf Valley to escape the bustle of a big city.

"Thanks." Lauren smiled.

"Did you hear about the senior center murder?" Zoe posed the question.

"No." Claire looked shocked.

"Should we talk about it in front of Molly?" Lauren asked.

"If we don't mention particular words we should be okay," Claire said. "I don't think she's paying attention, anyway."

Molly looked intent on spooning up the babycino, talking to Annie the whole time.

Zoe quickly told Claire about the hit and run, keeping her voice low.

"My goodness! And I thought we'd moved to a nice small town where these kinds of things don't happen."

"So did we," Lauren replied.

"Yeah," Zoe agreed. "Although it is rewarding trying to find out who did it."

"You two aren't going to get mixed up with this one, are you?" Claire frowned.

"We'll be careful," Zoe promised.

"I think the police have it all in hand," Lauren countered.

Zoe looked like she wanted to pout now. "But we're going to the senior center meeting this evening. Denise asked us to come up with some ideas for them in case they can't renew the lease with the new owner."

"And have you come up with anything?" Claire asked.

"Not yet," Zoe admitted.

"Me neither." Lauren gave a rueful smile.

"Hopefully the new owner will be nicer and leave the senior center alone," Claire said.

"That would be the perfect solution," Lauren replied.

They kept Claire and Molly company until more customers arrived. Annie stayed with the mother and daughter – ever since their first visit to the café, they'd become some of Annie's favorites.

The rest of the day grew busier, until Lauren didn't even have time to think of the upcoming senior center meeting.

"I can't believe it's five o'clock already!" Zoe sank down on a chair in the middle of the room. The last customer had just departed.

"I know." Lauren locked the door. If she sat down now, she didn't know whether she could get up again.

"At least we can rest our feet at the meeting this evening," Zoe said.

"Brrt." Annie jumped down from her bed and walked over to the door that led to the private hallway.

"You want to go home now?" Lauren unlocked the door and watched her saunter down the passageway until she met the cat flap. With a shimmy, Annie entered the cottage.

"I guess we'd better clean up." Zoe got up with a sigh. "And then get ready for the meeting."

"Should we have dinner first?" Lauren asked, her stomach growling.

"Good idea. If we call now, the pizza might arrive just as we finish up here." Zoe grinned.

Lauren ordered a sausage pizza, and was promised it wouldn't take long.

The thought of an early dinner spurred them on. Soon the hardwood floor looked clean and tidy with all the chairs stacked on the tables. Zoe turned off the droning vacuum.

"Time for pizza!"

Lauren looked out the window. A car pulled up outside their cottage next door.

"I think it's here."

Lauren and Zoe went outside and greeted the delivery driver.

One minute later, they were in the cottage kitchen, opening the large cardboard box.

"Brrp?" Annie asked as she wandered in from the living room.

"We're having dinner early," Lauren explained.

"Because we're going to the meeting tonight," Zoe added.

"Would you like something to eat now?" Lauren asked Annie.

"Brrt!"

Lauren opened up a new can of chicken with gravy and spooned it into Annie's bowl.

"I don't think pizza is good for cats," Lauren said regretfully.

"There are lots of food that isn't safe for cats," Zoe mused as she grabbed a large slice of pizza. The tantalizing aroma of the melted mozzarella and pizza sauce filled the kitchen.

"Brrp," Annie agreed sadly, before investigating her dinner.

Once they finished eating, they quickly got ready for the meeting.

"We shouldn't be too late tonight," Lauren told Annie, stroking her thick, velvety soft fur.

They drove to the center, the sky a pinky-orange as the sun set.

They were lucky to find a space to park as the lot was jammed with cars, including Denise's shiny blue vehicle.

"Everyone must be here," Zoe remarked.

A gleaming pewter colored minivan stood in the carport.

"I hope we're not late." Lauren turned off the ignition.

They hurried into the building. The place seemed deserted, until Lauren heard voices. Barry stood at the front of the same room as last time, speaking to a packed audience.

"Sorry," Zoe said as they entered.

"We haven't really started yet," Barry informed them. "Take a seat."

There were a few spare chairs left in the last row – the layout reminded Lauren of the church hall meeting.

She and Zoe said hello to Denise, Mrs. Finch, Hans, Ms. Tobin, Father Mike, and Martha as they walked down the aisle to the vacant seats.

"You might as well get started now, Barry," Martha called out. "The cupcake girls are here!"

There were a few chuckles.

"I think they forgot to mention our coffee," Zoe whispered to Lauren with a wink.

Denise got up from her seat in the front row and stood next to Barry.

"Yes, we should get started now," Denise echoed Martha.

"Very well." Barry nodded. "We haven't heard anything yet about who is the new owner of this property, I'm afraid. As soon as I know, I'll tell you."

There were a few groans.

"What about Crystal, the wife?" Martha asked. "She'll probably inherit."

"How do you know that?" a grumpy looking man asked.

"The wife usually does." Martha chuckled.

"We haven't been in contact with her," Barry stated. "I thought it would be best not to disturb her at present. She must have a lot to deal with."

"Yeah, like how to spend all her husband's money!" Martha was in good form.

"Has anyone come up with an idea in case we lose this building?" Denise took over. "Father Mike has been kind enough to confirm that we'll be able to use the church hall for some activities if we're kicked out of here, but we won't be able to have a fully functioning center at the hall."

"What about the crowd surfing idea?" a frail gray-haired woman asked.

"I think it's called crowd funding," Denise answered gently. "And I'm looking into that at the moment. But there are a lot of different sites online and we'll need to agree on which one to use. Even if we are successful and raise enough money to build our own center, we'll still need somewhere for our activities when we're in the construction phase."

"True," a few people muttered.

"More protests!" Martha called out. "I got a half price cappuccino for marching outside the café!"

"Me too!"

"It was good coffee."

"Now they're mentioning our coffee," Lauren whispered to Zoe with a smile.

"I got a swan on my latte!"

"Maybe the cupcake girls have got some ideas," Martha suggested.

A lot of the audience turned their heads toward Lauren and Zoe.

"Uh oh," Zoe muttered.

"I haven't come up with anything," Lauren murmured, shifting in her plastic chair.

"Lauren and Zoe?" Barry prompted.

Zoe stood up. "We don't have any new ideas. Sorry." She sounded regretful. "But on Tuesday we're having another half price coffee special between ten and eleven. Everyone's welcome."

There was a burst of applause.

"I can't wait to see Annie again," a woman wearing a pink jumper called out.

"I still think the crowdfunding idea is a good one," Zoe added.

"Thank you," Barry said.

"So let's get going with the crowdfunding," Martha directed.

"Denise?" Barry glanced at his assistant.

"I will get right on that and give you a report in two days' time," Denise promised.

"Let's talk about what really happened to Ralph," Martha proposed. "Since he was *deliberately* run over."

Half the people in the room inhaled in shock.

"I didn't know that!"

"Oh, my goodness!"

"I didn't like him, but I wouldn't have killed him."

"How does Martha know that?" Lauren whispered to Zoe. The only people she'd told about Ralph being deliberately run over was Denise and Zoe.

"I didn't tell her." Zoe mimed zipping her lips. "I haven't told anyone."

"Denise?" Lauren suggested. Would the no-nonsense assistant have gone around town telling everyone? Or had someone overheard her conversation with Denise in the café?

"Martha's a real livewire tonight," Zoe whispered to Lauren.

"You were out driving the minivan, Barry." Martha stood up, gripping the handles of her walker. "Did you see Ralph on the road before he was run over?"

"Of course not." Barry drew himself up.

"What time did you finish taking people home that night?"

"Ten p.m. I was busy dropping off people from just after nine until then."

Martha rummaged in her basket and pulled out a notepad and pen. She scratched something on the paper.

"What about you, Denise?" she asked.

Denise's mouth parted in a surprised O. "I was talking to you, Martha, and a few other members while Lauren and Zoe were packing up. Once all the guests left, I locked up and went straight home. You can check with my husband – he was waiting up for me."

Martha made another note, then grinned. "Just joshing with you two." She put the notebook back in the basket. "What about the cupcake girls?" Martha turned to the back of the room. "Lauren and Zoe. Someone told me you found him!"

Everyone stared at them.

Lauren cleared her throat. "Who – who told you?"

"Someone," Martha said mysteriously. She tapped the basket where she'd stashed the notebook. "Not much gets past me."

"The police are investigating," Lauren said.

Zoe nodded vigorously. Lauren half expected her cousin to blurt out they were too, but Zoe's lips stayed zipped.

"I think we should get this meeting back on track." Barry called everyone to order. "Lauren's right. The police are investigating. They told me so themselves."

"When was that?" Martha asked.

"The next morning," Denise spoke. "An officer contacted us and we told him what happened at the party the previous evening. I was shocked when I was told that Ralph Lapton had died like that. Shocked." She shook her head.

"Didn't you get the minivan washed the morning after the party, Barry?"

Martha persisted. "I drove past your house and you were washing the minivan, the same as you always do every Tuesday morning."

"That's right," Barry replied stiffly. "I'm sure everyone here knows how I like to keep the van clean and shiny. It's a good advertisement for the center. By the time I'd dropped off the last member at their house, I thought it would be easier to drive myself home in the van and bring it back here the next morning. I've done that before when we've had an evening function."

The meeting soon broke up after that.

"I don't think they decided on anything," Zoe muttered.

"Except to keep investigating your crowdfunding idea," Lauren replied.

Zoe stifled a yawn. "Let's go home."

"We could see if Mrs. Finch or Hans needs a ride," Lauren suggested.

They made their way to two of their favorite people who were busy talking to each other.

"Hi, Mrs. Finch," Zoe greeted her.

"Hi, Hans," Lauren said.

"Hello, Lauren, and Zoe," Hans replied. "How do you think the meeting went?"

"No one had any new ideas," Zoe remarked.

"True." Hans nodded.

"Perhaps Denise and Barry will use your crowdfunding idea, Zoe," Mrs. Finch told her.

"I hope so." Zoe brightened.

"Can we offer you two a ride home?" Lauren asked.

"That is very kind of you," Hans replied, "but Barry is driving us home."

"See you tomorrow, then," Zoe said.

"Make sure you come in next Tuesday for our half price specials," Lauren added. "If you can make it then."

"That is a generous offer of yours," Hans said. He lowered his voice. "Can you afford to do that?"

"Yes," Lauren assured him.

"We were run off our feet with the protestors' half price coffees," Zoe added. "And we made a nice profit!"

"Gut." Hans nodded.

"Can't wait for your coffee specials." Martha stopped on her way out.

"Annie might ask for another ride on your walker." Lauren smiled.

"That was fun." Martha grinned. "Tell her anytime."

"We will," Zoe promised.

"Oh, girls." Denise approached them as Martha departed. "I wondered if you could help me stack these chairs for a few minutes. Barry's attending to the minivan."

"Of course," Lauren said. Out of the corner of her eye, she could see the older people leaving the room.

Lauren and Zoe stacked the chairs alongside Denise.

"I'm so glad I asked you for help," Denise admitted when they were halfway through the task. Now the three of them were alone in the room.

"No problem." Zoe grinned. She surveyed the remaining twenty chairs. "The rest won't take us long."

"What do you think of Martha writing things down in her notebook?" Lauren asked. She'd been curious ever since she'd first seen Martha do so.

"Oh, she's been doing that as long as I've known her," Denise said. "She loves finding things out, particularly if it's a little salacious." She tsked. "I even caught her one day at the grocery store, buying one of those scandal rags."

"Oh, dear." Zoe sounded suitably shocked. A muscle twitched in her cheek.

Lauren wondered if her cousin was trying not to giggle, since she was guilty of the same offence.

"I do so hate it when Martha brings in those tabloids and shares them with the other members." Denise shook her head. "Of course, Barry lets her – he allows her to do whatever she wants – but if I was running this place, things would be different."

"In what way?" Zoe asked as she started stacking the last row of chairs.

"For a start, we would have more physical activities," Denise answered. "Like Pilates. It's so good for your core."

Lauren glanced at Denise's trim figure. Maybe she should consider trying something like that.

"Why don't you take over Barry's job when he retires?" Zoe suggested. "I know you said you worked here part-time but would you be interested in working longer hours?"

"To tell you the truth—" Denise looked around the room as if to double-check they were alone "—I would have loved to have Barry's job. I think I would have been a better director. More efficient. But he was already employed as the director when I started work here, and I soon realized he had no intention of leaving until he retired." She sighed. "And now my husband wants me to quit so I can enjoy myself while I'm still young enough. He's retiring soon and wants us to go on an extended cruise – around the world!"

"Wow," Lauren murmured.

"That will be awesome!"

"I am looking forward to it," Denise told them. "That's why I'm not applying for Barry's job when he finally leaves. It's just a shame I haven't been able to realize my full potential here."

They finished stacking the chairs, then said good night to Denise.

Lauren and Zoe walked out to the parking lot. Only Lauren's car and Denise's remained.

Once they were in the car, Zoe turned to Lauren. "That's a shame about Denise's frustrated ambitions."

"I know." Lauren nodded.

They discussed the meeting on the way home.

"Martha sure asked a lot of questions tonight," Zoe remarked. "And wrote things down in her notebook. Do you think she's investigating the murder?"

CHAPTER 6

Zoe's question had kept Lauren up half the night. Was Martha actually investigating Ralph Lapton's death?

The next morning though, Zoe seemed to backtrack on her theory.

"I think I got carried away last night," Zoe admitted at breakfast. "Maybe Martha wrote stuff down because she was taking the unofficial minutes. She might email all the members with her notes."

"That's one explanation," Lauren said, biting into her whole-wheat toast.

"Brrp?" Annie asked. She jumped on the chair next to Lauren's.

"We're wondering if Martha is investigating Ralph Lapton's death," Lauren told Annie.

"Brrt!"

"She is?" Zoe scrunched up her face.

"Brrt!"

"Huh. I think Annie has a good instinct for these sorts of things."

"Definitely." Lauren smiled at the cat.

"I hope Martha's going to be careful," Zoe said.

"Maybe we could have a chat with her when she comes into the café," Lauren suggested. "Tell her that murderers are dangerous people."

"For sure." Zoe nodded. "That's the only thing I don't like when we sleuth around – the murderer trying to get us!"

"Well, it shouldn't happen this time," Lauren said, "because we're not sleuthing around this time. Are we?"

Zoe wrinkled up her mouth as if debating how to answer.

"I wonder what happened at the vet's yesterday," Lauren tried to distract her cousin. "Ed was going to ask if anyone had reported AJ missing."

"That's right." Zoe poured granola into her bowl and a large amount of milk. "And I can't wait to find out what he says!"

***

The two of them burst into the café kitchen. Annie stayed outside the swinging doors, an inquisitive look on her furry face.

"I think Annie wants an update on AJ too," Zoe said.

"I'm sure she does." Lauren turned to smile at the silver-gray tabby before the door closed behind her.

"Well?" Zoe asked impatiently.

Ed looked up from a mound of dough.

"What did the vet say yesterday?" Lauren prompted.

"No one's reported AJ missing." Ed smiled briefly, then started pounding the dough. "And I checked the lost and found column yesterday and this morning, and nothing."

"I hope that means you can keep her," Zoe said.

"Me, too." Ed nodded. "The vet said they'll contact me if anyone enquires about her. I also visited the local shelter but nobody's looked for her there."

"I'll let Annie know." Lauren turned to go.

"Annie can visit AJ anytime she wants."

"I could be in charge of setting up the play dates." Zoe beamed.

"Let's open up." Lauren nudged her cousin.

"Thank Annie for finding AJ." Ed's smile transformed his face.

***

"String-art club night at Mrs. Finch's!" Zoe locked up the café at five o'clock exactly.

"Brrt!" Annie jumped off her bed and trotted to the door that led to the cottage.

"Don't you mean knitting, crochet, and string-art club night?" Lauren surveyed the empty room. They'd tidied up early, as the last customer had left a few minutes before five. "All we have to do is vacuum and then we can relax for a while."

"I wonder if Mrs. Finch will have any new craft suggestions for me," Zoe mused as she plugged in the vacuum.

"What about quilting?" Lauren teased.

"No." Zoe shuddered. "It involves sewing."

After cleaning the café, they had an early dinner of paninis and a raspberry swirl cupcake each. Annie had chicken in gravy, one of her favorites.

"Got your scarf?" Zoe asked as Lauren put on Annie's lavender harness.

"Yes." She glanced at the brown paper bag that held her knitting. Would she ever finish it?

They walked around the block to Mrs. Finch's house.

"Brrt!" Annie greeted Mrs. Finch when she opened the door.

"How lovely to see you, girls." Mrs. Finch smiled at all of them. "Come in, come in."

Once they were settled in Mrs. Finch's brown and beige living room, Lauren relaxing on the sofa, her red scarf in her lap, Mrs. Finch asked, "Didn't you bring your string-art, Zoe?"

"I need a new hobby," Zoe confessed. "And Annie—" she glanced at the cat, who sat on the floor next to Mrs. Finch, "—thinks I should give something else a try as well."

Lauren stifled a smile at the memory of Annie hiding Zoe's string-art threads under the sofa.

"Let me see." Mrs. Finch closed her eyes and furrowed her brow.

"Ooh, I know!" Zoe jumped up from the sofa. "String knitchet!"

"What's that?" Lauren wore a puzzled expression.

"I just made it up!" Zoe giggled. "What if I could bash nails into something – like a tube – and then I wrapped yarn around the nails to make a shape, sort of like string-art, but what comes out of the tube is a cross between knitting and crochet!"

"I've never heard of that," Lauren admitted.

"Oh dear." Mrs. Finch opened her eyes and frowned. "I'm afraid I have, Zoe."

"You have?" Zoe sounded disappointed.

"I had something like that once. It was called a Knitting Nancy. After winding the wool around the nails, a knitted tube would appear out of the other end."

"Oh, pooh." Zoe sank down on the sofa.

"Brrt?" Annie ambled over to her and placed her paw on Zoe's leg.

"It's okay, Annie. I thought I'd just invented a new craft and I haven't." Zoe sighed.

"What about making some bead jewelry?" Lauren suggested after a moment.

"Ooh." Zoe brightened. "I'd have to go and visit the handmade shop and see if they have supplies. I could make you something, Lauren. You, too, Mrs. Finch."

"That's very kind of you, Zoe." Mrs. Finch gestured to the string-art picture of a pink flower on a black fabric canvas on the opposite wall. "I love looking at what you created for me."

"That's what I'll do," Zoe declared. "Investigate bead jewelry." A shadow crossed her face. "I hope it doesn't involve a lot of banging."

"I think Annie and I will be okay with a tiny bit of banging," Lauren said, hoping it was true.

Lauren knitted a few more rows while Zoe and Mrs. Finch discussed the developer's death.

As she slipped the last stitch from her needles, Lauren stared at her red scarf.

There was only a few inches of wool left in the skein.

"I think I've finished." Her voice was hushed.

"What?" Zoe looked over.

"Brrt?" Annie jumped upon the sofa next to Lauren and patted the red woolen garment with her paw.

"I've finally finished knitting this scarf!" She held it up so her cousin and Mrs. Finch could see her creation.

"That's wonderful, dear." Mrs. Finch beamed at her. "It looks very nice."

"Yes, it does," Zoe said. "You've done it! You could wear it on the way home."

"Definitely." Lauren stroked the scarf, relishing the feel of the fuzzy softness against her fingers.

"Now you can make one for Mitch," Zoe teased. "The weather's getting a little cooler now and if you start right away, you could finish it for Christmas!"

"Another one?" Lauren sank back on the sofa, the comfy cushions against her back. "But ... I've just finished this one."

"I bet he'd love a handmade gift from his girlfriend." Zoe giggled.

"Yes ..." Lauren's voice trailed off as she looked down at the scarf. There were a few holes in it, as it was the first thing she'd ever knitted, and at times she'd wondered if she would ever finish it. She'd chosen garter stitch, which Mrs. Finch had suggested as the easiest stitch to master.

Pride flickered through her. She'd actually completed it.

But she couldn't give Mitch a scarf that had even one hole in it. What if she knitted Mitch something and he didn't like it? He wouldn't say so of course, but ...

"Maybe Lauren needs a little break before she starts a new project," Mrs. Finch said.

"Yes." Lauren looked at her gratefully.

"Brrt," Annie added.

"Okay." Zoe nodded. "But we could go to the handmade shop on Monday and you can look at yarn, and I can look at beads."

"That sounds like a good plan." Mrs. Finch nodded. "Just looking at wool doesn't mean you have to start something right away."

"All right." Curiosity flitted through her. What sort of yarn would the little shop have?

They used Mrs. Finch's pod machine to make coffee for all of them, then said goodbye before it got too late.

Lauren wrapped her red scarf around her neck before they left the house.

"It does look good on you, Lauren," Mrs. Finch told her.

"Thank you." Lauren smiled.

"It's a shame we can't sleep late tomorrow," Zoe said as they walked home. She suddenly stopped in her tracks and clapped a hand over her mouth. "Oh, no!"

"What?" Lauren halted, her eyes wide as she stared at her cousin.

"Brrt?" Annie did the same.

"I forgot to make posters for our Tuesday specials next week!"

"I forgot too!"

"Don't worry." Zoe patted Lauren's arm. "I'll whip up some when we get home."

"What about tomorrow at breakfast?" Lauren suggested.

"As long as I remember." Zoe tapped her head. "I can't believe I forgot."

"We've had a busy week," Lauren replied. "What with catering the senior party and—"

"—someone killing Ralph, the new landlord." Zoe nodded. "And trying to come up with solutions in case the seniors are kicked out of their center."

"No wonder we forgot."

"Brrt!"

CHAPTER 7

At breakfast the next morning, Zoe whipped up a poster on the laptop.

"It looks pretty good." Zoe pressed Print. The whir of the printer started.

Annie stared in fascination at the paper coming out of the device.

"Brrt?" She jumped up on the kitchen table and pawed the white piece of paper.

"We're offering half price coffees on Tuesday," Lauren told Annie as she chewed on her granola.

"Maybe we'll get some new customers." Zoe showed Lauren and Annie the notice.

Half Price Tuesday!
Half price coffee, tea, and hot chocolate between ten and eleven Tuesday morning.
Tell your friends!

"We should see if we can post one at the senior center," Lauren suggested.

"That is genius," Zoe replied. "I know we told them about it at the meeting, but maybe there are members who weren't able to attend. Now they'll find out they can get a discounted latte!"

"Let's go after we close today," Lauren said.

"Good idea. And then I'm going to research bead jewelry online."

"And I'm going to read my book." Before she got ready for her date with Mitch.

Soon after, they opened the café. Zoe stuck one of the posters in the window. "This is sure to bring us some customers on Tuesday."

Lauren hoped they would be extra busy that day, but also hoped her feet wouldn't be as worn out as the day they'd run the half price protestor special.

The morning passed by in a blur. When she wasn't serving customers, Lauren thought about her upcoming date with Mitch.

"I'm pooped!" Zoe flopped on the stool behind the counter. The last customer had left and they'd made quick work of cleaning up.

"So am I," Lauren admitted as she locked the door. She was also starving.

"I can't believe so many of our customers asked about the new Tuesday specials." Zoe beamed. "I bet it's going to be huge!"

"Good thing we've got plenty of coffee beans, then."

"I'd love a mocha right now, but I can't be bothered to make one," Zoe confessed.

"I know the feeling."

"Brrt?" Annie padded to the door leading to the cottage.

"We have to go to the senior center to put up a poster," Lauren told her as she unlocked the door. "But when Zoe and I get back, we can relax all afternoon."

"Brrt!" *Good.*

Annie trotted down the private hallway and pushed her way through the cat flap.

"Let's get going." Zoe heaved herself to her feet and grabbed a brown paper bag from behind the counter. "I saved us two paninis for lunch."

"Awesome." Lauren smiled. Now she and Zoe didn't have to prepare anything for lunch.

They jumped into Lauren's car and drove to the senior center.

"We'll just ask Barry – or whoever's on duty – for permission to put up the poster, and then we can go home," Zoe said as Lauren parked in the lot.

Only a few cars were there, including the minivan.

"Maybe they don't have any scheduled activities right now," Zoe mused as they entered the building.

"Hello, Lauren, and Zoe." Barry suddenly appeared in front of them, wearing a button-down gray shirt and brown trousers. "What can I do for you?"

"We'd love it if we could put this sign up about our Tuesday specials." Zoe thrust the flyer at him.

"Of course." Barry scanned the notice. "Sounds like a good deal for our members. We can pin it up on the board."

They followed him down the hall until they came to a large corkboard covered with posters for upcoming events.

He tsked as he took down three flyers. "Out of date. I don't know what Denise does when she's on duty. It's her job to keep this board current."

"Oh," Lauren murmured.

"Maybe she's been busy looking into crowdfunding," Zoe suggested.

"Maybe." He sounded doubtful. "It was a good idea of yours, Zoe, but I just don't know how feasible it would be. We would need a block of land close by so all of our members can still attend. I can pick up folks, but if the new center is too far out, it's going to cost more in gas. But let's see what happens."

He pinned their notice to the board. "There. I'll make sure our members see your offer."

"Thank you," Lauren said.

"So what are you two up to for the rest of the day?" he asked. "You didn't bring Annie with you?"

"No, she's having a break right now," Lauren replied.

He chuckled. "I will be too, in a couple of hours. In fact, I'm going to get my vegetable patch ready to plant some spinach and Swiss chard."

"Really?" Zoe looked surprised.

"I love gardening when I have time for it. And if I have any surplus veggies, I bring them in and share them with our members."

"That's very kind of you," Lauren said.

"What else am I going to do with them?" He shrugged. "A lot of people my age grew up on home grown fruit and vegetables, but now it's not so easy for them to grow their own food. At least this way they're still getting vitamins and minerals from fresh veggies."

He escorted them to a large room that had comfortable looking sofas and armchairs.

"This is our library," he said proudly. Oak bookshelves lined the walls. "We have a lot of gardening magazines and books if you two are interested in the subject."

"Thank you, but I don't have much time for gardening because of the café," Lauren said. She hadn't even mowed her lawn lately – Mitch had done so.

"But we do have an herb garden," Zoe piped up.

"Wonderful." Barry beamed, then his expression changed. "What is this doing here?" He picked up a fashion magazine from the coffee table near them. Underneath were gardening magazines.

"Problem?" Zoe asked.

"Denise again." He shook his head. "She knows I like to keep the magazine topics separate from each other. The fashion magazines belong on that coffee table over there." He gestured to the other side of the room.

"I can take it over there," Zoe offered.

"Thank you." He placed the magazine in her outstretched hand. "I'm sure Denise does these kinds of things on purpose."

"Really?" Lauren frowned.

"I think she's always wanted my job." He chuckled without mirth.

"But she's retiring soon. Just like you." Zoe zoomed back from the other side of the room.

"She is?" Barry's eyebrows rose. "How do you know that?"

"Oops." Zoe unzipped her lips.

"We don't know for sure what Denise's plans are," Lauren hurriedly said, giving Zoe a warning glance. "Do we?"

"That's right." Zoe nodded vigorously. "Not for sure."

"If she's leaving, then I need to know about it." Barry frowned. "So I can advertise for a replacement."

"You might be retiring before she does, though." Zoe put in.

Barry seemed disgruntled at the thought.

"We'd better go." Lauren nudged Zoe.

"Yep. Thanks for letting us put up our poster."

They waved goodbye and hurried out of there.

"Me and my big mouth." Zoe shook her head as she jumped into Lauren's car. "I hope Denise doesn't find out what I let slip just now."

"Me too."

***

That night, Lauren and Mitch had dinner at the Italian restaurant at Zeke's Ridge.

Over their meal of lasagna and mushroom risotto, she told him she'd finally finished knitting her scarf.

"That's great." He smiled across the table. "Why aren't you wearing it? You're going to show me, aren't you?"

"Of course," she replied, warmed by his interest. She'd debated wearing it that evening, but had eventually decided it didn't quite go with her teal dress. "I'll show you back at the cottage."

"I'll hold you to that." His dark brown eyes were warm.

Yes, she was totally going to knit him a scarf for Christmas – one that didn't have any holes in it.

Afterward, Lauren enjoyed watching an action adventure movie with Mitch. The seats were plush and comfortable, and his arm around her shoulders was reassuring. The theater was only half full, and she had a great view of the screen. She was a little sorry when the movie finished, and their cozy cocoon was no more.

Mitch drove her home and walked her up the porch steps.

"Come in and you can see the scarf," she told him.

He followed her inside, her senses attuned to his close proximity.

There was no sign of Zoe and Annie – were they hiding somewhere, spying? Or were they going to jump out and surprise them? Sometimes she wouldn't put anything past her cousin.

"It's in here."

He followed her to the living room.

The garter stitch scarf lay across the sofa.

"Brrt?" Annie asked sleepily. She was curled up next to the woolen garment.

"Hi," Lauren said softly.

"Hi, Annie," Mitch said.

"Brrt," Annie replied. She studied the two of them for a moment, then closed her eyes, as if dozing off again.

"Here it is." Lauren picked up the scarf and wrapped it around her neck.

"It's good." His smile was full of approval.

"It is? But there's a hole here, and one there." She felt compelled to point out the mistakes. "And another one down here." Her finger jabbed at the annoying error.

"You put a lot of effort into it," he told her. "Don't be so hard on yourself."

"I'll try," she promised.

He leaned in to kiss her. Zoe's faint giggle down the hall barely registered.

***

On Monday, the one weekday the café was closed, Lauren and Zoe visited the handmade shop.

"Oh, look." Zoe swooped toward the bead section. "Orange, and pink, and red – and yellow! How am I going to choose?"

Lauren barely heard her, because her attention was focused on all the different types of yarn. Should she buy pure wool, a wool/acrylic blend, or just acrylic? She wanted Mitch's scarf to be warm and cozy, and not scratchy.

"Hello," a woman with curly brown hair greeted them. "Zoe, do you need any help?"

Zoe explained her bead jewelry dilemma, adding that Lauren needed to buy some yarn to make her boyfriend a scarf.

The clerk recommended to Zoe that she start off slow, only buying what she needed immediately, and helped Lauren choose a wool/acrylic blend yarn that was soft and snuggly, in a fawn hue.

"Mitch is going to love it," Zoe assured her as they left the shop.

Lauren peeked into Zoe's paper bag. Her cousin had chosen pink and gold beads, some leather cord wire, and a silver clasp.

"I think you're going to make an amazing bracelet," Lauren told her.

"I hope so." Zoe grinned. "Maybe this will be my new thing."

***

The next morning, Lauren and Zoe sat down to breakfast extra early.

"It's good that you called Ed yesterday and asked him to work an extra hour this morning." Zoe grabbed the slice of whole-wheat that had just popped up from the toaster and slathered butter on it.

"I didn't want anyone to be disappointed if all of his pastries sold out quickly," Lauren explained. "But …" she paused "… what if our half price specials today are a big flop?"

"Then we can offer Father Mike the left-over pastries and cupcakes," Zoe replied. "I'm sure he can put them to good use."

Lauren nodded as she crunched on her granola.

"But I bet it will be a huge success," Zoe continued. "Just like our half price special for protestors was last week."

"Brrt?" Annie wandered into the kitchen. She jumped up on the wooden chair next to Lauren's and peered at the cell phone next to the bowl of granola.

"We'll be opening the café soon," Lauren mumbled around her cereal.

"Brrp." Annie hooked her paw around the phone and brought it toward her. "Brrp!" She pressed a button.

"What are you doing?" Lauren's eyes widened.

"Brrt, brrt, brrp!" Annie spoke to the phone.

On the other side of the line, a faint "Mew!" sounded.

"Who are you talking to?" Lauren glanced at the screen.

"Who?" Zoe leaned across the table.

"She's called Ed," Lauren replied.

"You mean she's called AJ." Zoe giggled. "How is AJ, Annie?"

"Brrt." *Good.*

"Mew, mew, mew!" came from the phone.

"Who is this?" Ed's gruff voice sounded from the other end.

"It's Annie," Lauren called out. "She's saying hello to AJ."

"I'll be at the café in a few minutes, Lauren," Ed spoke. "AJ's fine. She's really settled in."

"That's great," Zoe shouted toward the phone.

"Ed has to go, Annie." Lauren indicated the phone. "Do you want to say goodbye to AJ?"

"Brrt, brrt," Annie said.

"Mew, mew," AJ replied.

***

"I checked at the vet's again yesterday," Ed told them when they arrived at the café. A tray of apple Danishes was already in the oven. "No one's reported a missing kitten matching AJ's description. And nothing in the lost

174

and found newspaper column either. So I'm keeping her."

"Awesome!" Zoe grinned. "I bet Annie will be happy to hear that."

"If she doesn't know already," Lauren said. "Maybe that's what she and AJ were talking about over the phone."

"Tell Annie she can call AJ anytime." Ed smiled – a rare occurrence. "If I told anyone what I'd heard, I don't think they'd believe me."

"Unless they knew Annie was involved," Zoe said.

***

Their half price coffee specials were a big success. Lauren and Zoe were slammed with customers the minute the clock hit ten. A lot of them were members of the senior center.

"Hi, gals." Martha appeared at the *Please Wait to be Seated* sign, pushing her walker. "Where's the cutie pie?"

Annie trotted over to greet her. She patted the black seat of the walker. "Brrt?"

"Hop on!" Martha slowly pushed the walker toward the tables as Annie kept her balance on the seat. "Tell me where to sit."

"Brrt!"

Ms. Tobin, Hans, Mrs. Finch, and Father Mike visited. So did Denise and Barry. Annie had directed Martha to a large six seater, and had chosen which customers could sit with her. This included Denise, Father Mike, and three ladies that Lauren recognized from the party at the senior center.

Martha talked and laughed with her tablemates, occasionally jotting things down in her notebook.

"I told you today would be successful." Zoe beamed with pride as she surveyed the full café. They'd made lattes and cappuccinos practically nonstop for the last hour.

"Luckily Ed made extra pastries." Lauren surveyed the empty glass case that usually held the cupcakes and pastries. Only three cupcakes remained. "We've sold them all so far."

"But he's got two more batches in the oven," Zoe told her. "And I've already put our names on two of them."

"Good thinking." Lauren smiled.

She glanced over at Martha's table. Barry stood next to the senior, talking to her and the others at the table. Martha wrote something down in her notebook, then said something to her tablemates, laughing as she did so.

"I wonder what Martha's up to?" Zoe followed Lauren's gaze.

"I hope she's not investigating the murder."

"But I think *we* should," Zoe said. "Let's talk about it later today."

The morning raced by. Some of the customers lingered, opting for a second coffee at full price, even though Lauren offered them the half price discount again.

Lauren and Zoe got a short break at lunch, when they were able to cover for each other. They weren't as busy; Zoe reasoning that some of the lunch crowd came during the morning instead so they could get a bargain coffee.

Lauren knew without counting the receipts that they'd made a decent profit that day already.

She had a quick lunch in the cottage, making do with some toast, fruit, and the pastry that Zoe had earmarked for her.

When she came back from her break, Annie dozed in the cat bed. Only one-third of the tables were occupied.

"You could have taken longer," Zoe told her as Lauren joined her behind the counter. "It's been pretty quiet."

"After this morning, I don't mind fewer customers." Lauren eased onto the stool and wiggled her feet.

"Maybe we could do this every week – or every second week," Zoe suggested. She gestured to the tip jar next to the register – it was stuffed full with dollar bills and silver coins. "Ed and I are going to be very happy today."

Since Lauren owned the café, she didn't think it was fair she took a share of the tips. She paid Zoe and Ed a decent wage, and the tips were a little extra for them.

"I guess I'd better be going, girls." Martha pushed her walker to the counter.

"I must owe you a lot of money. I had a good time here today." She looked over at the cat bed. "I think your cute gal is all tuckered out, though."

"I'm glad you enjoyed yourself." Lauren found the bill.

"I'll definitely come back." Martha handed over some cash. "Half price lattes is a great idea. Everyone's talking about it at the center."

"Awesome!" Zoe beamed.

Lauren opened the door for Martha and watched her trundle out of the shop.

"Bye." Lauren waved to her.

Martha waved back, then pushed the walker forward down a slight incline. The walker kept rolling forward. Martha's mouth opened in surprise as she struggled to keep up.

"Help! I can't stop!"

CHAPTER 8

Lauren rushed out of the café, closely followed by Zoe.

"What's wrong?" Lauren ran to catch up with Martha.

"The brakes aren't working," Martha gasped. She held on to the handles of the walker, the skin stretched tight across her knuckles as she labored to keep up a running pace.

Lauren and Zoe grabbed the handles of the walker.

"There." Zoe grunted. "Stopped."

"Thanks." Martha breathed heavily.

A couple of passersby looked at them curiously, a man coming over and asking if they needed help.

"I think we'll be okay," Lauren told him, thanking him.

"What happened, Martha?" Zoe asked.

"Lemme sit down." Martha sank onto the vinyl padded seat. "Don't let go of the handles or it will take off down the hill – with me on it!"

The "hill" was a slight incline, but Lauren suspected Martha was suffering from shock.

"Can you make it back to the café?" Zoe said. "You should have a rest."

"I've been resting all morning," Martha replied. "Wanted to make sure I didn't miss out on your lattes, then I had a cappuccino, and then a pastry. Then I thought I'd stay awhile after everyone left, and check all my notes." She patted the seat of the walker. Under the lid was a basket.

Was that where Martha kept her notebook?

After a minute, Martha continued, "I usually brake before the sidewalk goes downhill so I'm prepared for the next bit. But when I pressed the brake handle, nothing happened. I thought this bad gal was going to run away with me all the way down the hill." She shuddered. "I didn't realize there was something wrong with the brakes because I usually forget to put the brakes on when I park it somewhere, like at your café." A guilty looked flashed across her face.

"If you're up to it, I think you should come back to the café," Lauren suggested gently. "We could make you a cup of hot, sweet tea, on the house."

"Or hot chocolate," Zoe added. "That has sugar in it as well. And maybe you need a cupcake or a pastry, if there are any left. Our treat."

"That sounds good." Martha smiled, but it wasn't her usual confident smile.

"How did this happen?" Lauren asked. "Are the brakes defective?" She pressed the brake lever attached to the handle but nothing seemed to happen.

"Someone cut my brakes. And I think it was Denise!"

***

"Why would you say that?" Lauren asked. The three of them now sat at a table in the café. Annie jumped on a chair and gently patted Martha's arm, as if she knew the senior had suffered a shock.

"Thanks, cutie pie." Martha smiled at Annie, then turned to Lauren. "To answer your question, I don't think Denise likes

182

me. She always acts so judgey about my choice of reading material."

"You mean gossip magazines?" Zoe asked.

"Yep. Why shouldn't I read something entertaining? And I'm sure some of those stories are true. You know what they say – no smoke without fire."

"Definitely." Zoe nodded.

"But why would she tamper with your brakes?" Lauren frowned. "I thought she enjoyed working at the senior center."

Martha shrugged. "I don't know who else it could be. And she was right here with me this morning, sitting at the same table. We even had an argument about whether it was true that an actress had plastic surgery. I said it's so obvious, but Denise got all hoity toity about it and said she was sure this actress hadn't touched her face at all."

"Huh." Zoe rose. "What can I get you? You definitely need something for the shock."

"A hot chocolate would be nice," Martha said. "With marshmallows."

"Coming right up." Zoe hurried to the counter.

"Would you like a cupcake or pastry?" Lauren asked.

Annie looking enquiringly at Martha, as if waiting for her answer.

"No thanks, girls," Martha replied. "I'm good."

"How are you going to get home?" Lauren asked. "You can't use your walker if the brakes aren't working."

"I'll call Barry. I'm sure he can pick me up." Martha opened the seat lid of the walker and rummaged around. She brought out a red flip phone that had large buttons on the keypad. "I've got his number on here."

"Tell me if he can't make it." Lauren surveyed the café. Only a few tables were occupied. "I could take you home if we don't get any busier."

"You're a sweet gal." Martha beamed. "So is your zippy cousin. Lemme know if she needs any help in the romance department and I'll fix her up."

Zoe brought over the hot chocolate, Lauren filling her in on Martha's transport options.

"Barry says he can come get me." Martha waved her phone in the air. "He'll be here in thirty minutes, which will give me plenty of time to drink this cocoa." A satisfied expression flickered across her face. "Lots of marshmallows. Goody."

The surface of the drink was invisible due to the multitude of pink and white marshmallows Zoe had crammed into the mug.

Annie kept Martha company while Lauren and Zoe attended to the counter, taking payment from a few of the customers.

Barry collected Martha, helping her to the minivan parked outside. He came back for her walker, tsking at the fact the brakes weren't working.

"Don't worry," he told Lauren and Zoe. "I should be able to fix it for her back at the center. We have several of these walkers – some as spares, and some we're keeping for the parts. If I can't fix the brakes, I can give Martha a loaner."

"That's good of you," Lauren said.

"Yep." Zoe nodded.

They waved goodbye as Barry and Martha drove off.

"What a day," Zoe said. "And it's not even five o'clock yet."

"I know." Lauren sank down on the stool behind the counter. Our of the corner of her eye, she could see Annie settling down for a snooze in the cat bed.

"Do you think we could close early for once?" Zoe asked hopefully, eyeing the clock. "If we don't have any customers. It's three now."

"That's a good idea," Lauren said. Normally she'd feel guilty about doing so, but not today. "Want a mocha with extra chocolate powder?"

"Now you're reading my mind." Zoe grinned.

"I'll make them." Lauren ground the beans and tamped them down in the portafilter.

She wondered if Mitch would stop by this afternoon. She hadn't seen him since Saturday night. Just thinking of the way he'd kissed her after she'd shown him her scarf made her eyes flutter closed and a dreamy smile grace her lips.

"Hi, Mitch," she heard Zoe sing out.

Her eyes snapped open.

"Hi." She hoped what she'd just been thinking wasn't written all over her face.

"Hi." Mitch stood at the counter.

In her cat bed, Annie lifted her head, and welcomed him with a sleepy, "Brrt."

"Remember I said I might have a friend who'd like to meet Zoe?"

"Yes," Lauren replied.

"Yes!" Zoe jumped off the stool.

"He'll be here in a second."

The door to the café opened and a tall guy in his late twenties strode in. His features were even and attractive, and he wore jeans and a navy t-shirt.

Zoe blinked. "You!" She pointed at him, her mouth hanging open.

"You!" The guy froze mid-stride, staring at Zoe.

Lauren looked at her cousin and then the newcomer, comprehension dawning. "You!"

"Would someone tell me what's going on?" Mitch frowned. "Chris, have you already met Zoe?"

Zoe, Lauren, and Mitch's friend all spoke at once.

"He—"

"She—"

"He—"

Annie jerked her head up at the altercation, then buried herself in her blankets, her paw over her eyes.

"Do you have a brother?" Zoe finally said, her face turning crimson.

"Yes." The newcomer grimaced. "And I'm sorry. I had no idea he did that until after I came home. I've been overseas."

"So your brother used *your* photo on an internet dating site to attract women." Lauren's eyes narrowed. She remembered how upset Zoe had been when she'd discovered the deception a few months ago.

"Your eighteen-year-old brother." Zoe's eyes looked like they could steam a latte from twenty yards.

"What's going on?" Mitch turned to his friend and then back to Zoe and Lauren. "What are you all talking about?"

"I went out on a date with his brother," Zoe explained, her tone icy. "I thought I was going out with *him*." She pointed to Mitch's friend. "But when I got to the restaurant, his eighteen-year-old brother was there instead, and told me how he liked older women. I'm only twenty-five!"

The newcomer winced.

Lauren wrapped her arm around her cousin's shoulders.

"That was the last straw." Zoe leaned into Lauren's hug for a second, then straightened her spine. "I don't think I will ever internet date again!"

"I'm sorry," Mitch's friend repeated. "I've dealt with my brother and he'll never do something like that again. I didn't realize when Mitch said I might like to meet his girlfriend's cousin that it was you."

"Does that make a difference?" Zoe narrowed her eyes.

"Of course not," he assured her hastily.

"Maybe it isn't the best time for this," Lauren told Mitch. "We could talk about it later, after I speak to Zoe about it."

"Sure." Mitch grabbed his friend's arm. "I think you're right. Let's all take some time to think this through." He urged his buddy out of the café.

"Ooh – ooh!" Zoe stomped behind the counter.

Luckily there were only a couple of customers at the rear, and they hadn't seemed to notice the drama.

"The nerve of him!" Zoe banged down an empty milk jug on the counter.

"Mitch's friend – or his brother?" Lauren asked. Then wished she hadn't.

"Either. Both." Zoe banged the stainless-steel jug again.

Lauren was sure she could hear her cousin grind her teeth.

After a moment when there wasn't any more commotion, Lauren ventured, "Feel a little better?"

"Just a bit," Zoe admitted. "Sorry." She sank down on the stool.

Lauren glanced over at Annie. She'd opened her eyes and was staring wide-eyed at Zoe. But she hadn't left her basket.

Zoe sighed – a long, drawn out one.

"Why does this happen to me? I was hopeful that this – this friend of Mitch's might be—" she lowered her voice "—you know – the one – *maybe* – and it turns out to be *him*! Someone with a horrible, juvenile brother who steals his photo and impersonates him." Zoe's face reddened again.

"I get it. I do," Lauren said. "You have every right to be angry. But Mitch didn't

190

know his friend's brother did that to you. It happened before he and I started dating."

"I know." Zoe sighed again. "Mitch is a good guy. You're lucky."

"Maybe his friend Chris is a good guy, too."

"Hmmph." Zoe's grunt made it sound like she didn't believe it.

"Why don't we talk about something else?" Lauren suggested. No other customers had come in since Mitch and Chris. Annie had settled down once more. Maybe Zoe was right and they should close as early as possible today.

"Martha." Zoe perked up slightly. "You know, she offered to fix me up with a nephew or someone." Her face dimmed. "I might have to take her up on her offer – eventually."

"What do you think about Martha's brakes failing?" Lauren asked, trying to keep her cousin's mind off romance.

"We should definitely look into why she thinks Denise tampered with them," Zoe said. "Also, how Martha might be investigating the murder. That's our job." She sounded like she wanted to pout.

"Maybe we could do some snooping around," Lauren offered. She didn't think it was a great idea, but it might cheer up Zoe. And the police hadn't arrested anyone yet for the crime – or if they had, they were keeping it very quiet.

"Yeah!" Zoe jumped up from the stool. "Let's visit Denise after we close the café. We could tell her about Martha's brakes and see what she says."

"All right. Do you know where she lives?"

"No, but I bet the Internet does." Zoe tapped some buttons on her phone. "There's only one listing for Hamrick for Gold Leaf Valley." She showed Lauren the screen. "I saw Denise's last name on the noticeboard, where they had a schedule for the staff and volunteers."

"Her address isn't far from here."

They ended up closing the café just after four. Annie ran down the private hallway to the cottage, had a few mouthfuls of beef in gravy, then wandered into the living room, where she curled up on the couch.

"She's had a busy day." Lauren gazed at the silver-gray tabby for a moment.

"We shouldn't be long, Annie," she said softly.

"Brrp." Annie lifted her head for a second, then nestled into the sofa cushions with a contented sigh, closing her eyes.

Lauren and Zoe walked the few blocks to Denise's address, which turned out to be a royal blue Victorian house. Since the town originated from the Goldrush era, many houses in the area were of that time.

A shiny blue compact car was parked in the driveway.

"That's Denise's car." Zoe nudged Lauren.

"Good. She should be home."

"I guess she likes the color blue."

They walked up the narrow path to the front door. A small, neat lawn surrounded them on either side.

Lauren heard the doorbell chimes ring inside the house.

Footsteps sounded, and then the front door was opened.

"Lauren, and Zoe." Denise seemed a little harried. She wore beige slacks and a rose top.

"Hi," Lauren said.

"Hi." Zoe sounded chipper. "We're not disturbing you, are we?"

Denise hesitated. "No." She shook her head. "What can I do for you?"

"Do you think everyone enjoyed themselves at the café today?" Zoe asked. "With our half price specials?"

"I'm sure they did," Denise replied with a little smile. "It's so good of you girls to do something like that."

"When Martha left the café today, the brakes on her walker failed. She nearly crashed down the hill."

Lauren pressed her lips together at Zoe's exaggeration.

"Oh, my." Denise's eyes widened. "That's terrible. Come in." She beckoned them to follow her down the hallway painted in cream with pearl gray accents.

Denise led them to the living room, decorated in shades of cream and robin's egg blue. "Please, sit down." She gestured to a three-seater sofa.

Lauren and Zoe sat, while Denise sank into a matching armchair opposite them.

"Poor Martha. Is she okay?" Denise asked.

"I think so," Lauren said, when Zoe didn't speak. She glanced around the room, noticing what she suspected her cousin had. A suitcase was laid out on another armchair, with clothing strewn over the back of the chair.

"Are you going somewhere?" Zoe asked.

"What? Oh." A slow tide of pink suffused Denise's face. "Please excuse the mess. I was sorting out clothes for my upcoming cruise."

"But I thought you weren't going right this minute," Zoe said.

"True," Denise replied. "But it never hurts to get things done a little early. And there will be formal dinner clothes I need to pack, as well as casual outfits. And I need to leave room for souvenirs." She laughed. "I have to pack my husband's suitcase as well. You know how men are. If I left it to him, he'd only pack two shirts and they'd be totally crushed. People would think I don't look after him!"

There was a short silence.

"But enough about me," Denise said. "Tell me more about what happened to

Martha. Are you sure her brakes failed? She's always leaving that walker around with the brakes off. Maybe she thought they were on when they were actually turned off."

"She said the brakes wouldn't work," Zoe replied.

"I tried it myself when we wheeled it back to the café. Nothing happened when I pressed the handle to turn on the brakes," Lauren added.

"Oh dear." Denise shook her head. "Martha loves that walker. She should be able to get it fixed, though. Maybe Barry could—"

"Yep, he's going to repair it," Zoe told her.

"Oh, good." Denise looked relieved. "Can I offer you girls something to drink? I've only got instant coffee, I'm afraid, but there's juice and water in the fridge."

"Thank you, but I think we should get going." Lauren rose. "We've had a busy day."

"Of course." Denise rose as well.

Lauren flicked a look at Zoe. Her cousin scrambled off the sofa.

They said goodbye to Denise and walked out onto the street.

"We could have grilled her for a bit longer," Zoe complained once they were out of earshot.

"About what?" Lauren asked. "We couldn't accuse her of cutting Martha's brakes."

"Couldn't we?" Zoe raised an eyebrow, then sighed. "No, you're right. We couldn't. Not unless we were totally confident, and had evidence that she did it."

"And we don't."

"No." Zoe sounded regretful. "But don't you think it was strange she was packing? I know she said it was for her cruise in the near future, but what if she was planning to leave town right now? Because she killed Ralph?"

CHAPTER 9

"But why would Denise kill Ralph?" Lauren asked as they turned into their street. There weren't any passersby, so she didn't think their conversation could be overheard. "Because she was upset that he was going to close down the senior center?"

"Exactly." Zoe pointed a finger at her. "She was so angry about it, that she killed him. Or maybe she told him, *"Continue the lease on favorable terms and I won't kill you."* And he laughed at her. And then, BAM! She killed him."

"By running him over?"

"She got in her car after he laughed at her, and then ran him over."

"But Denise said she was talking to Martha and a few others while we were packing up after the party that night," Lauren pointed out. "And then she said she went straight home."

"Well, there is that," Zoe reluctantly admitted. "But do we know for sure that she went straight home? Don't forget,

Martha was writing things down in her notebook. Denise was there this morning, sitting right next to her at the cafe when she was jotting things down. Maybe she got worried about what Martha was writing in her journal, so she thought she'd better take care of her."

"I think of Denise as efficient, but not capable of doing something like that," Lauren said slowly.

"But has she done anything about crowdfunding for the center?" Zoe asked as they walked up the porch to their cottage. "We haven't gotten an update from her about it. She was going to look into it last week, wasn't she? And then update everyone on her research."

"What about Barry?" Lauren asked as they entered the cottage. "He's the director. Shouldn't he be in charge of sourcing funding if they need to move to a new place?"

"Maybe he's delegated it to Denise," Zoe said as they walked into the living room.

Annie was still curled up in a ball on the sofa.

"Shh." Lauren touched her finger to her lips.

"Ohhh." Zoe's voice was soft. "Let's go into the kitchen."

They tiptoed past Annie. Once they were sitting at the kitchen table, Zoe continued.

"Barry might have told Denise to look into the crowdfunding because maybe he's not good on the computer – or the Internet. Or he might be too busy running things and driving the seniors around to have time to research it."

"But Denise said she'd look into it at the meeting."

Zoe shrugged. "Because she knew he was too busy. Or not good on the computer. And if she wanted it to get done, she knew she'd have to. Like packing her husband's clothes for the cruise – if that's what she was going to do and it wasn't just a lie."

"So you think Denise is a suspect," Lauren said.

"Yep. And Barry. He was pretty upset about the developer's big announcement at the party."

"That seems so long ago." Lauren shook her head.

"I know. And it was only last week!"

***

The next day, Wednesday, Lauren gave Annie the day off.

"Brrt." She sounded pleased at the idea.

They were all at the breakfast table, Annie sitting on the chair next to Lauren.

"What do you think you'll do today, Annie?" Zoe asked.

"Brrt!" Annie jumped off the chair and trotted out of the room.

"Maybe she's going to play with her toy hedgehog," Lauren suggested.

"Or push my string-art threads under the sofa again," Zoe joked. "It's okay, I don't mind her doing that because now I'm beading!"

"How's it going?"

"I haven't started, yet," Zoe admitted. "We've been so busy with our half price specials and everything, that I haven't had time. But maybe tonight I can get going with it."

Before they left for work, Lauren found Annie sleeping on her bed. She lay on her back, her silver-gray tummy on full display. Lauren's heart filled with love as she gazed at her.

***

Business was slow but steady that Wednesday morning.

"Maybe everyone came in yesterday," Lauren said as she surveyed the one-third full café.

"And they might have overcaffeinated themselves," Zoe added. "Oh well, we can treat ourselves to one of Ed's pastries for lunch."

"Good idea." Lauren placed two apricot Danishes into a paper bag. "For us."

Zoe grinned, then her expression changed. "Oh, look. Crystal!"

"Where?"

But Zoe was halfway out the door.

Lauren watched through the large café window as her cousin hailed the young widow. Today, Crystal's strawberry blonde hair was pulled back in a ponytail, and she wore expensive looking jeans and a clinging jade sweater. Zoe and Crystal spoke for a moment, then Zoe ushered her into the café.

"Have a latte on the house." Zoe smiled at Crystal, then gave Lauren a look that said, *I'll explain later.*

"Where's your cat?" Crystal looked around the café and the occupied tables. "Wherever I go in this town, people are always talking about her."

"She's having a day off," Lauren told her. "Zoe will find you a table."

"This way." Zoe guided Crystal to a table near the counter, where the neighboring tables weren't occupied.

Lauren made the latte, the hissing of the milk wand providing a backdrop to the low buzz of conversation from their customers.

"I hope you like it." Lauren placed the coffee with a peacock design in front of Crystal.

"Oh, wow." Crystal's eyes widened. "I haven't seen a design like that in Sacramento – apart from one café there."

"That must be Amy's," Lauren said. They'd taken an advanced latte art class there a couple of months ago and learned how to make swan and peacock latte art.

Crystal took a sip and sank back into the wooden chair. "I think I needed that. I've just been to the senior center and spoken to Barry. My lawyer said to let him take care of things, but I thought going in person might help make up for the distress my husband caused with his big announcement."

"What did you say to him?" Zoe leaned across the table.

"Zoe," Lauren hissed.

"It's okay. I inherited the center, as well as most of my husband's property." Crystal took another sip. "I don't know if I was imagining things, when I told you I thought he was looking around for a new wife, or if he hadn't had time to change his will. But I have to wait for probate to go through before I can access the money."

"So?" Zoe prompted.

"So I went to talk to Barry, to tell him the senior center was safe. I'll renew the lease on the same terms as before, for as long as they want."

"But your husband made it sound like the big hotel was practically a done deal," Lauren said.

"Not really. He had partners lined up, but they hadn't gotten development approval or anything like that yet. Who knows?" Crystal shrugged. "It might never have gotten approved anyway—" she hesitated "—unless he was able to approach the right people. My husband liked to boast about his achievements, sometimes before they'd even happened."

"That's very good of you to renew the center's lease," Lauren said.

Crystal smiled. "I like that old lady, Martha. She nearly got me with her rolling walker on the night of the party. She reminds me of my great-aunt."

"So what will you do now?" Zoe asked.

"I'm going to sell the house in Sacramento – although I might have to fix the height level on the barn first, because of the neighbors, which will be a pain. My lawyer's handling that for me. But once the money comes through from probate, I'm going to Hawaii for a while."

"Hawaii?" Lauren asked.

"I went there once on spring break when I was in college," Crystal replied. "I loved it. I wanted to go there on my honeymoon, but Ralph said he didn't have time for one, he was too busy negotiating some deal. So I'm going now. No one can stop me." She looked fierce.

"What about your cabin here?" Zoe asked curiously.

"I'm going to keep it – for now." Crystal stirred her half full latte. "If I come back from Hawaii, I might want somewhere I can just chill for a while. And I know I can get a good meal at Gary's Burger Diner. And great coffee here, of course," she added.

She spoke for a few more minutes about her upcoming trip to Hawaii, then thanked them and left.

"Well." Zoe stood behind the counter, her hands on her hips. "Huh."

"What does "Huh" mean?" Lauren asked. No customers had come in during Crystal's visit, so she sank down on a stool next to Zoe.

"I think she's the killer." Zoe kept her voice down.

"What?" Lauren reared back to eye her cousin. "I was thinking the opposite."

"What?" Zoe sounded shocked.

"If she killed her husband, wouldn't she want to continue with the mega resort deal her husband was making?"

"But she's fleeing to Hawaii," Zoe pointed out.

"The FBI could bring her back here. It's not as if she's moving to another country in the middle of nowhere which doesn't have an extradition treaty with the U.S."

"Isn't she?" Zoe scrunched up her nose. "She *told* us she was going to Hawaii. What if she's really flying somewhere else? Somewhere without extradition?"

"I'm sure the authorities will check that out," Lauren said.

"You can ask Mitch," Zoe suggested. It sounded like an order.

"Yes, I can. But Crystal said she was waiting for probate to go through. So she's not going anywhere yet."

"That we know of!"

***

"Let's visit Barry," Zoe announced that afternoon. "We can see if he's fixed Martha's walker. And find out what Crystal told him about the new lease for the center."

"Okay," Lauren replied. She was glad their investigating seemed to be helping take Zoe's mind off her drama with Mitch's friend, but would they learn anything new from Barry? She didn't know who her lead suspect was.

Lauren locked the front door at five o'clock on the dot.

"Do you think Barry will be at the center or at home at this hour?"

"Let's try his house first." Zoe pressed the buttons on her phone. "It might be closer than the center." A minute later: "I've found his address! He's only a couple of blocks away from Denise's house."

"We could take Annie for a walk." Lauren vacuumed the hardwood floors while Zoe cleaned the counter. "She might like some fresh air after being home all day."

"Good thinking." Zoe grabbed her phone. "I'm ready."

"So am I."

They trooped down the private hallway to the cottage. Annie sat in a kitchen chair, facing her toy hedgehog on the table.

"Brrt?"

"Want to go for a walk with us?" Lauren asked.

"Brrt!" Annie hopped down from the chair.

"You'll have to wear your harness," Lauren warned.

"Brrp." Annie's mouth formed a pout.

"We're going to visit Barry," Zoe told her. "From the senior center."

Annie looked interested as Lauren buckled her into the lavender harness.

"Let's go!" Zoe led the way out of the house.

A few passersby stopped them on their way, wanting to say hello to Annie.

"We should check on Mrs. Finch," Lauren said as they rounded the corner into Barry's street. "She didn't come in today."

"Good idea," Zoe said. "We could visit her on the way home. Annie would like that, wouldn't you?"

"Brrt!" Annie's plumy tail waved in the air.

They walked along the sidewalk until they reached Barry's Folk Victorian house, a simpler and smaller version of the typical Victorian house in Gold Leaf Valley. An attached garage, painted in the same pale yellow, was closed. There was no sign of his car or minivan.

"Maybe he's not home." Lauren furrowed her brow. She didn't know if this was a good idea or not.

"We won't know until we try." Zoe marched up the path to the front door and rang the bell.

A faint *ding dong* echoed through the house.

No one came to the door.

Zoe pressed the bell again.

"If he doesn't answer this time, I think we should leave," Lauren said. "Maybe he's at the senior center."

"All right." Zoe chewed her lip. "Ooh, maybe he's in the garden. Remember he told us he likes growing veggies?"

Zoe left the porch and walked around the front garden to the left. A tall wooden fence with a gate blocked their view of the backyard.

"Hello?" She called out. "Barry?"

"I'm back here," a man's voice called out. "Come through the gate."

"Come on." Zoe pushed back the bolt and opened the gate.

"Brrt?" Annie looked up at Lauren.

"Zoe wants to talk to Barry," Lauren told her.

Annie followed Zoe, towing Lauren.

"Hello, girls." Barry straightened up from his vegetable patch. He wore old brown trousers and a white shirt. Small green plants that looked like spinach dotted the rectangular piece of soil. "What can I do for you?"

Lauren waited for Zoe to take the lead. She didn't have to wait long.

"We bumped into Crystal today," Zoe said, seeming to forget that it was she who had encouraged the widow into the café. "She said she'd given you good news for the senior center."

"She has indeed." A big smile spread across his face. "I've already posted a notice on the board, and I've told the rest of the staff and the volunteers to give everyone the great news."

"How's Martha's walker?" Lauren asked.

"I managed to fix it." He shook his head. "Someone cut the brake line. Terrible."

"It certainly is," Zoe agreed. "Where's your car? We didn't see one parked outside."

Lauren frowned at her cousin's nosiness.

"It's in the garage." He chuckled. "My doctor said my blood pressure is a bit high and I should lose some weight." He patted his paunch. "So I've been walking to the center."

"That's quite a distance," Lauren said.

"It takes me about thirty minutes." He looked pleased with himself. "I don't know if I'll stick with it, though. I'd rather drive to work and spend my free time in the garden." He gestured to the veggie patch. Green lawn took up the rest of the garden apart from some shrubs near the back fence line.

"I see you're into composting." Zoe glanced at the big pile of grass clippings, and fruit and vegetable peelings at the end of the bed of soil.

"I'll have to get a composter," Barry said. "I think the heap has started to attract a few mice – or other creatures."

"Oh, no." Lauren took a few steps away from the pile.

"Annie wouldn't let a mouse get you, would you, Annie?" Zoe grinned at the cat.

"Brrt!" Annie seemed to agree.

"Can I offer you two something to drink? I was just about to go in and grab a glass of water." He mopped his shiny face with a handkerchief. "I'm afraid I've been out here a while and I'm starting to feel it."

"We're fine," Lauren told him. "But thank you."

"Yep." Zoe nodded. "Maybe we should get going. Oh, we've decided to have another half price coffee hour next Tuesday."

Lauren shot her cousin a look. *We* have?

"So it would be great if you could tell all your members," Zoe finished.

"I will." He smiled. "I'm sure some of them will be happy to hear that."

They said goodbye and watched him go into the house through the back door.

"I think we should go," Lauren said, "and discuss half price coffee."

"On the way to visit Mrs. Finch," Zoe said in an unconcerned tone.

"Brrt!"

"Yes, we're going to visit Mrs. Finch next," Lauren told Annie.

Annie sniffed around the compost heap.

"Brrt!" She pawed at something at the bottom of the grass clippings, hooking it out.

"What have you got there?" Zoe bent down to look. "Lauren," she whispered. "Quick!"

"What is it?" Lauren squatted down. Her eyes widened as she looked at the small piece of purple glass. Her mind flashed to the scene of the hit and run. On Ralph's wrist had been a smashed watch, the glass casing shattered – the exact distinctive shade of this fragment.

She straightened up and looked at Zoe.

"It was Barry!" They spoke at the same time.

"Let's get out of here." Lauren picked up Annie. "And call the police!"

"Not so fast." Barry suddenly loomed in front of them. "I knew I should have gotten rid of that piece of glass – the senior center would have been the perfect place to dispose of it in the trash – far too many suspects for the police to deal with. But I actually thought it would be safer to bury it at the bottom of my compost pile." He laughed harshly. "I watched you just now from the kitchen window. I saw what you found."

Annie's ears flattened.

"I knew there was a reason we suddenly didn't see your car around," Zoe told him. "You're getting it fixed, aren't you? At some shady chop shop in the middle of nowhere, to repair the damage you did running over Ralph."

"You watch too many crime dramas." Barry shook his head. "I didn't use my car. I used the minivan."

"But – you're still driving it around," Lauren said.

"After the … accident, I checked the bumper for damage. I couldn't see any. That van is tough. I checked again early the next morning, which is the day I always get it washed anyway, and decided to clean it myself. I couldn't see any blood – or anything else on it. Nobody suspected a thing."

"But what is the piece of watch glass doing here?" Lauren furrowed her brow.

"I have no idea." He tsked. "I didn't discover it until I got home and changed my clothes. I washed them, just in case there was a hair fiber or something caught, and that's when I saw the glass on my trouser leg. I got out of the van after I hit him to make sure he was dead."

"But you said you had an alibi for the time of death," Zoe pointed out.

"Yes." He smiled. It wasn't a nice smile. "When I got out of the van to check on Ralph, I changed the time on his watch to an earlier time in order to give myself an alibi, wiped my fingerprints, and then smashed it with my wheel brace. The police thought the time of death was the time on the watch."

"That is … genius." Zoe stared at him, appalled.

"Isn't it? At the fake time of death, I was driving the seniors home, and they're my witnesses."

"But … what was Ralph even doing there, on that side road?" Lauren asked.

"I slashed his tires – two of them – in the parking lot," Barry replied. "I was so angry when he announced he wasn't going to renew our lease and was going to build a mega resort instead, that when I went outside to get the van ready to take my members home, I slashed his tires. That's all I was going to do." His face twisted.

"What happened?" Lauren clasped Annie to her. The feline purred in a low rumble that sounded dangerous.

"I was driving back to the center. I'd dropped off everyone and I was going to park the minivan in the carport, then go home in my car. I lied to Martha about that at the meeting. Then I saw Ralph's fancy car." Barry paused. "He'd managed to pull over in the side road and was peering at one of his damaged tires. Something just came over me and I drove straight at him. He shouldn't have tried to take the center away from me. I told him how much it meant to me – us – at the party, and that the seniors would be displaced if he went ahead with his plans to build a resort, but he didn't care. He laughed at me!" Barry sounded like he still couldn't believe that.

"The senior center is my life. I've been so happy there – apart from some niggles with Denise – I mean, she still hasn't provided me and the members with a list of crowdfunding options, not that we need it now – and I realized right then I had the power to try and save our place from greedy people like him. So I took care of him."

Lauren stepped back. She sensed Zoe did, too. Rage bristled off Barry.

"We're the good guys," Zoe told him. "We gave your members half price coffees."

"But you know too much!" He took a step toward them.

Lauren now stood next to the compost heap. She gave Zoe a desperate sideways look. Annie vibrated in her arms, her growling purrs louder. She'd have to place Annie on the ground in order to give her last-ditch plan a chance to work.

"What about Martha's brakes?" Zoe asked suddenly. "Did you cut them?"

"Yes. She loves writing down gossip in that notebook of hers. I didn't like the way she questioned me at the meeting at the center, asking me if I had an alibi for the time of Ralph's death. I hoped she'd stop poking around, but when I saw her talking to the other members and writing things down in that journal at your half price coffee hour, I knew I had to do something."

"I never suspected it was you," Lauren said.

"When I fixed Martha's walker, I told her maybe the killer had done it, and she should let the police do their job. She tried to laugh it off but I could tell she was a bit shaken by the incident. I didn't think she was going to be a problem anymore – but you girls are!"

He lunged toward them.

Annie jumped out of Lauren's arms and landed at the edge of the compost pile. She dug at the grass clippings and fruit peelings, the debris arcing up into the air and heading toward Barry.

It was as if Annie had read Lauren's mind. She followed Annie's lead and grabbed a huge handful of the compost and flung it into Barry's face.

Zoe zoomed to the other side of the rotting pile and copied Lauren's actions.

"Ow! Yuck! Stop it!" Barry covered his eyes. His face was covered in green lawn clippings and a rotting banana peel hung off his nose.

They didn't stop. They chucked huge handfuls of waste at him, Annie's legs and paws working furiously as she tunneled through the pile, the compost spraying up behind her and onto Barry's waist and chest.

"Let's go!" Lauren threw one more handful at Barry's face, then grabbed Annie.

"I'm with you!" Zoe hurled a wad of grass clippings at him, hitting him square in the chest. "Run!"

Lauren held Annie tight to her chest as they ran out of the back garden and onto the street.

"We should have brought the car," Zoe panted, leading the way home.

Lauren kept up with her cousin, spikes of adrenaline helping her as she clutched Annie and ran for their lives.

Halfway home, Zoe stopped for breath.

"Is he behind us?" she panted, pulling her phone out of her jeans.

Lauren turned. "No," she gasped.

Annie's paws were on Lauren's chest, and she looked inquiringly at her. "We need the – police," Lauren managed.

"Brrt!"

Zoe punched the buttons on her phone and was connected to an emergency operator. Sucking in air, she quickly explained what had happened.

"We have to get out of here," Zoe said, shoving the phone back into her pocket. "In case he comes after us."

They raced home, Lauren putting Annie down on the carpet, and locking the front door. Panting, she checked the back door was locked, too.

"Maybe I should start going to the gym," she attempted to joke as she flopped down on a kitchen chair.

"I think I'll join you." Zoe's face glowed with exertion.

"Brrt!"

EPILOGUE

Not long afterward, the police visited their cottage. They'd apprehended Barry, who was still trying to get the grass clippings and vegetable peelings out of his hair when they'd arrived at his house.

After taking their statements, the police left.

"I can't believe it was Barry." Zoe poured two glasses of water.

"Me neither." Lauren shook her head.

Annie nudged her arm. She'd been sitting next to Lauren at the kitchen table, but now she climbed into her lap, wanting a cuddle.

"You were amazing, Annie." Lauren stroked her velvety soft fur.

"Definitely." Zoe nodded.

"Brrt!" Annie sounded proud.

"I wonder who will run the senior center now?" Lauren mused.

"Martha?" Zoe suggested. "What about Hans? Or Ms. Tobin? She goes there sometimes."

"I guess we'll have to wait and see."

***

They didn't have to wait long. The next day, Denise entered the coffee shop. Mrs. Finch had already been in and they'd updated her on their sleuthing.

"Brrt?" Annie looked up sleepily from her basket before ambling over to the *Please Wait to be Seated* sign.

Lauren had encouraged Annie to take the day off but she had insisted on coming to the café that morning. Had she known Denise would stop by?

"Wonderful news, girls." Denise smiled down at Annie, then walked toward the counter. "You're looking at the new director of the senior center!"

"That was fast." Zoe spoke.

"I know." Denise shook her head. "I can't believe Barry killed Ralph – and you girls – the three of you – confronted him!"

"How do you know that?" Zoe asked.

"The police came to my house last night and told me what had happened." She looked at them in admiration. "That

224

was very brave of you, visiting a murderer."

"We didn't know he was one at the time," Lauren told her.

"I've now been offered Barry's position – and I'm going to take it! Although I can't decide yet whether I want to be the director temporarily or permanently." She beamed.

"But what about your cruise?" Lauren asked.

"And your husband's retirement?" Zoe added.

"My husband said he's pleased I'm so happy right now, and he doesn't mind if we delay our cruise for a few months. I've got a little vacation leave saved up anyway, so if I decide to take the job permanently, we'll still be able to go away. It won't be the extended around the world cruise that my husband hoped for, but when I do retire, we can go on a long cruise then."

"That's wonderful," Lauren said.

"Brrt!"

"It's strange how things work out, isn't it?" Denise pondered. "Yesterday I'd finished writing up a list of crowdfunding sites, and was going to present it to Barry this morning, but before he left work he'd put a note on my desk saying we didn't need to move as Crystal was renewing the lease for us."

They congratulated her once more and offered her a latte on the house, but Denise insisted on paying full price. "I can't wait to get my next paycheck – it will be for a lot more than usual!"

A few minutes after she left, Mitch strode in.

"Why didn't you call me last night?" he asked Lauren. "I was investigating a burglary at Zeke's Ridge, but I would have come over as soon as I could."

"I'll leave you two to it. Annie, I'll ask Ed how AJ is doing." Zoe turned toward the kitchen.

"Brrt!" *Good.*

"Zoe, my friend Chris says he owes you dinner. You can name the place and time," Mitch told her.

"Hmm." Zoe looked like she was going to dismiss the offer, then paused. "Tell him I'll think about it."

Zoe pushed open the swinging kitchen doors and disappeared. Annie waited outside.

"You know I'm always here for you," Mitch said softly to Lauren.

"I know." She smiled. And she did know.

They gazed at each for a long moment, then Zoe hurried out of the kitchen.

"Annie, Ed says AJ's doing well. Would you like to have a playdate with her?"

"Brrt!" *Yes!*

The End

Please keep reading for a list of all my titles!

I hope you enjoyed reading this mystery. Sign up to my newsletter at http://www.JintyJames.com and be among the first to discover when my next book is published!

AUTHOR NOTES

Annie is based on my own Norwegian Forest Cat, who was also called Annie. Annie was my second cat. AJ is based on my first cat who was called AJ. They didn't meet each other in real life, but now they have in story form!

Zoe's disastrous Internet date with Chris's brother was detailed in Purrs and Peril -A Norwegian Forest Cat Café Cozy Mystery – Book 1

A list of all my books is on the next page!

TITLES BY JINTY JAMES

Have you read:

Purrs and Peril – A Norwegian Forest Cat Café Cozy Mystery – Book 1

Meow Means Murder – A Norwegian Forest Cat Café Cozy Mystery – Book 2

Whiskers and Warrants – A Norwegian Forest Cat Café Cozy Mystery – Book 3

Maddie Goodwell Series (fun witch cozies)

Spells and Spiced Latte - A Coffee Witch Cozy Mystery - Maddie Goodwell 1

Please note: Spells and Spiced Latte should be free on Amazon. If it's not, please contact me via Facebook (I'm on it nearly every day) or email me at jinty@jintyjames.com

Visions and Vanilla Cappuccino - A Coffee Witch Cozy Mystery - Maddie Goodwell 2

Magic and Mocha – A Coffee Witch Cozy Mystery – Maddie Goodwell 3

Enchantments and Espresso – A Coffee Witch Cozy Mystery – Maddie Goodwell 4

Familiars and French Roast - A Coffee Witch Cozy Mystery – Maddie Goodwell 5

Incantations and Iced Coffee – A Coffee Witch Cozy Mystery – Maddie Goodwell 6

Made in the USA
Middletown, DE
21 March 2023

27291414R00139